T0063245

Jester and Zara

Robert Pfister

authorHOUSE®

AuthorHouse™
1663 Liberty Drive
Bloomington, IN 47403
www.authorhouse.com
Phone: 1-800-839-8640

© 2015 Robert Pfister. All rights reserved.

No part of this book may be reproduced, stored in
a retrieval system, or transmitted by any means
without the written permission of the author.

Published by AuthorHouse   01/08/2015

ISBN: 978-1-4969-6206-5 (sc)
ISBN: 978-1-4969-6205-8 (e)

Library of Congress Control Number: 2014922960

Any people depicted in stock imagery provided by Thinkstock are models,
and such images are being used for illustrative purposes only.
Certain stock imagery © Thinkstock.

This book is printed on acid-free paper.

Because of the dynamic nature of the Internet, any web addresses or
links contained in this book may have changed since publication and
may no longer be valid. The views expressed in this work are solely those
of the author and do not necessarily reflect the views of the publisher,
and the publisher hereby disclaims any responsibility for them.

Contents

Author's Foreword

Since I was seven years old, I've had a passion for monsters. My father would drop my little brother and me off at the movies, usually a Godzilla double feature matinee. Toys and models of monsters adorned my room. Many books filled with creatures both real and imagined, lined my meagre bookshelf. I was fascinated with how (and what) they ate, crushed, burned, or otherwise destroyed in their wake. To this day, I'm still enjoying the monsters that either creep or crash into our lives. My favourite, of course, is the dragon. Powerful, magical, the ability to fly, and their fiery breath! What's not to like?

Acknowledgements

I'd like to thank these people for their kind words
of encouragement, creativity, and personal time
they have so graciously given on my behalf.
Tara Cameron
Enid Rodriquez
Loa Ross
Kelsey, Ken and Ted Pfister

Chapter One

(And so it begins)

The fields were burning. Everything as far as the eye could see, was ablaze now. The livestock, all the farm's buildings, were engulfed in flame. The dragons, controlled by Vectus, had done their job well. The war had gone his way for almost a year. His invasion from the sea had caught the kingdom of Tyde almost completely unawares. The confusion was exactly what he had hoped for. His kind of evil magic had asserted itself everywhere the battles had been fought. The scores of black dragons had destroyed everything in their path. Vectus himself thrived on evil. He was a true warlord of Ionicus, a dark land of barbaric rulers since time began. It was take or be taken! His corruption of all things living in his own kingdom would now extend here for eternity. His troops were well trained, and fearless. Any resistance was met with ruthless attacks. Thousands had been either killed or enslaved. It was a policy of leaving nothing worth keeping.

Vectus was in his command shelter when the first bad news came. One of his commanders entered the large tent and was seriously injured. He did not want to be the one to give the news. Vectus turned and regarded the commander. His armour had been partly melted on one side. He had been burned rather terribly on his back and right side, clear to his foot. "Too close to the dragons I see. What was it that had you so close to them?" he asked. "Not them, your darkness! It was an attack on us! All the dragons in our group are no longer…Only I and three others from our section made it back alive." said the now terrified commander. "All the dragons? That's impossible! You will tell me exactly what happened!" Vectus knew the commander was telling the truth, but wanted to hear what happened anyways. Just then, another commander burst into the tent. "Sir, the, the dragons sir, they are lost! We are being pushed back to the sea!" the commander fell to the ground. His entire backside was burnt to the bones. Vectus stared; it was definitely dragon fire that had done the damage. He made a mental note of that. It had to be another type of dragon. One he had not researched. An unknown breed perhaps! He looked at the other commander, who was in great pain, but waiting to tell his account of what happened. "Speak, commander. Leave nothing out!" he ordered. The commander removed his helmet and ran his hand over the top of his head. "Sir, they came from nowhere. They fly in small groups and attack all at once. You yourself said a dragon will not attack another. I've seen it with my own eyes! The little ones took fully half our dragons, maybe more." The commander looked at the sand on the ground. "Little ones?" Vectus was surprised at that. He rarely was surprised anymore. "Are you talking of children, or dragons?" Vectus asked in an agitated voice. "Dragons sir. Little dragons. No larger than a young dog. Extremely fast, and very deadly. Their fire was a colour I've never seen before, a very pale blue. Hard to see, but far worse than our dragons!" the commander coughed and went silent. "I want more details commander, think carefully before you speak again" said Vectus. "Sir, they always come from out of the sun. Extremely fast moving and in groups only. Our dragons were on fire before they knew what was happening. S…sir, I thought dragons were immune to dragon fire? Even from other dragons, they burned all the way to the ground. The small ones would then dart away so quickly, then regroup and attack again. Very organized and very deliberate sir. I can't describe them well, far too fast to get a good look. Small, and greenish, and as fast as lightening sir." The commander exhaled and stared at the sand again. "If what you are telling me is correct, then these 'little ones' are being controlled by someone I have yet to meet. Go now and complete your duties. Say nothing of what you have seen to anyone. Leave me." Vectus turned from the commander and went to his map table. Little green ones indeed.

Something was up, and it was changing the flow of his invasion plans. He was not happy. As the commander left his tent, a commotion began out side. Men were yelling and running. Vectus strode out of the tent in time to witness one of his own large black dragons, completely engulfed in flames, crash into the men and equipment on the beach! A second dragon, it too, burning and dying slammed into the ground near his tent. The heat from the fire was more intense than anything he had known before. The armour he wore became very hot suddenly. His own tent began to burn. Vectus ran for his maps as a third dragon, also in flames took his tent and everything in it as it hit the ground hard, then bounced and flipped onto its back. Vectus had no choice but to run for the longboats. The heat from the dragon bodies was so intense; there was no air to breathe! The shallow water along the shoreline in places was beginning to let off steam. He got into one of the longboats and willed it to move out from the shore. As the beach receded, two more dragons met their sad end on the beach. There was too much going on and he was having trouble maintaining his control over the remaining dragons. Vectus squinted into the distance. His dragons were falling from the sky as far as he could see. His troops, too small in numbers could not defend against the well trained and still plentiful troops from Tyde. They were pushed back into the sea. Those that could get on longboats lived, most never made it that far. Vectus was incensed. How could a few small dragons burn his dragon-armada from the sky? He turned to the landmass that was Tyde and outstretched both arms. He summoned dark grey clouds. The sun disappeared behind them. He looked straight up and mouthed the words only he knew and understood. His eyes rolled back up into his head leaving only the whites exposed. The ground rumbled and lightening raced across the sky sideways. A heavy wet snow began to fall. In moments it was a full on blizzard. The temperature began to fall to well below the freezing point. The winds increased to near hurricane force. Slowly the land disappeared in a heavy frozen cloak of whiteness. Vectus set sail back to Ionicus. This was by far from over.

The chosen ones released their power of the little green dragons. Most were dead from the sudden and intense cold. It had caught them in their one weakness. For all their speed and intense flame producing ability, the sudden, drastic drop in the temperature was their undoing. A few lingered on in the great inland forest but the cold even got to them. The thousands of displaced villagers returned to their burned lands and salvaged what they could. The clouds began to thin out and the sun finally returned to Tyde. The land holders freely gave out there stockpiles of seeds for the next crops. It would take time to rebuild.

Chapter Two

(The seed is sewn)

The forest was alive with every manner of chirping birds, chattering squirrels, rustling sounds in the undergrowth, some nearer than others. It was the sheer volume of the sounds that woke Jester from a sound sleep and the annoyance of a dream interrupted. Jester opened one eye. The thin predawn light foretold of nights last dying moments before slipping away. The dawn's promise of light was at hand. To Jester, it felt like all the forest's creatures were in this very room! He opened his other eye, half expecting the see the sources of the racket at his bedside. The dim light allowed him to see only a huge tangle of clothing all over the floor. Two full suits of dented armour, one still propped up in a corner, the other face down on the stone floor. His slightly bent sword hung precariously from the wardrobe handles, about to fall to the floor at any moment. Suddenly, the forest noise stopped dead! He could only hear his own heart beat now. He got up from the bed and crossed to the tall window that looked out on the great forest. Complete silence. Puzzled, he turned and rummaged through the clothing all over the floor and managed to find an almost clean tunic and a pair of leggings. Dressed, he grabbed a pair of well worn boots and his sword. He descended the stone steps towards the courtyard. The place was filled with rows of market stalls where buyers and sellers bartered for goods from all corners of the kingdom. The smell and smoke from cooking fires made him hungry. Banners and flags hung still, waiting for a breeze to bring them to life. His troops, locals, and travellers alike crisscrossed the cobbled yard unawares of the silence out side the gates. Unnoticed, he exited the castle wall through a short narrow door hidden from view by a large creeping vine that very nearly reached to the top of the battlements. He used this door when by himself. It was intended to be used as an emergency escape only.

The strangely silent forest was only a hundred feet away. A well worn path leading deep into the trees was just visible in the rapidly approaching sunrise. Jester walked a ways into the forest by this path, then turned into the trees and proceeded as quietly as he could till he came to a large clearing occupied by knee high grasses. On any given morning, stags and their harems would be grazing the grass in this very spot. It was devoid of wildlife now.

He paused, as he thought he could hear the first sound not of his own making, it was someone running! He stepped just behind a great gnarled tree trunk and waited. A moment later, a woman burst into the clearing! She wore a plain long grey dress and had a hooded robe tied loosely at her waist. She paused briefly, glancing behind her, and proceeded to the center of the clearing. She was carrying what looked like a large loaf of bread with her, held to her chest as if it were an infant. Jester was about to reveal himself when suddenly, a great rush of air parted and flattened the grasses in the clearing! Above, a huge dragon was just flaring its great wings and landed with a deep thud, which Jester felt beneath his feet! The massive wings folded against its sides. It had to be nearly ninety feet from head to tail! And he was sure it had to weigh as much as his entire troop, horses included! The dragon lowered its head towards the woman as if a servant would to its master. Jester was in awe! He'd only seen a few dragons in his lifetime. He knew they were of dark, but not always evil magic and very deadly when provoked or surprised. As a young man he had heard the stories of dragons from the old story tellers. It gave him goose bumps then, even a few sleepless nights! He knew there were different types of dragons too, but had no idea which kind this might be. What was even more startling, was a dragon in the company of a human. This was the largest he had ever seen! Especially this close! Although he was a warrior and a leader of men, he felt fear for the first time in quite awhile. He was now concerned for his own safety and that of the woman's, even though she seemed acquainted with the beast.

The woman gently placed the 'loaf' onto the ground and put her hand on the great beasts lowered head. She spoke to it, but Jester could not make out the words, just the monsters steady breathing. The woman stepped back slightly as the dragon carefully picked up the oblong in its jaws. Jester watched transfixed by what came next! The dragon lifted its head straight up. Nearly twenty feet of neck alone, he guessed, as if to swallow the 'loaf' whole. Instead, a rush of yellow-white flame erupted from its mouth! The 'loaf' at the center, was blasted by the flame. Jester could feel the intense heat from where he stood. He watched as the flame changed colour to a very intense blue, creating even more heat if that was possible! A moment later, the great dragon gently placed the object back onto the ground. The grass sizzled and popped, then began to burn. The flames spreading quickly! Neither dragon, nor the mysterious woman made any attempt to flee the fire! Jester could not just stand there and watch any longer!

A troop of men from his castle rode up just behind him at that moment to see the fire and its cause. Jester grabbed the first startled man and pulled him from his horse! He snatched the lined chain mail blanket of the wide eyed animal and ran towards the fire without further thought. He wrapped the chain mail blanket haphazardly over his head and shoulders. It would only offer a brief protection from the grass fire. The men looked at each other but were unsure of their own safety with the dragon so close at hand! Jester could not breathe as he ran headlong through the flames! Just as he felt he could go no further, he was past the wall of fire and crashed into the surprised, open mouthed woman! They both fell heavily onto the ground by the dragon's clawed feet. The dragon roared in anger but could not tell Jester or the woman apart in the heap of blanket tumbling on the ground. It shot straight up; great wings spread, and left the clearing. Jester grabbed the woman in the blanket and ran for the trees! She hung from his shoulder, occasionally bumping against tree trunks and scraggly branches. He came to a second smaller clearing and dropped the struggling bundle to the ground. He bent and pulled the blanket off the incensed woman. She looked at him and punched him full on the nose with all her might! Jester heard and felt his nose break. He held his nose with both hands as the blood began to run. The woman got up quickly and was swinging her second punch, but jester caught it in his hand and pulled her onto the ground, his left knee gently pinning her shoulder. His troop's had made their way into the second clearing and were surprised to see the scene before them. Jester released the woman, who ran a few steps toward the men yelling, "Arrest this man! I want him flogged on the spot!" She turned to face Jester, who was still holding his nose, and crossed her arms. The troop's sergeant was closest to her. He leaned forward and said to Jester," You alright sir? You gave us a bit of a start when you ran off like that. Young Ives back here, well sir, he was wondering if you still have his horse blanket." All the men laughed. The woman was undeterred and faced the sergeant. "I demand you arrest this, this man, and have him flogged! I will not tolerate his unwanted manhandling of me!" She turned back to Jester. He rolled his eyes. Infuriated, she lunged at him again. He easily sidestepped her and again gently pinned her to the ground! The troop unsheathed their swords as one. "Hold fast!" yelled the sergeant. "I, for one, believe he can hold his own here!" The men laughed again.

Jester was almost face to face with the woman. She was really very beautiful. And strong too! She struggled but could not shake him off. "My dear lady, ill let you back up only if you can behave yourself. This isn't the polite way to thank me for your rescue from certain death back there." She stopped her struggles, and cautiously, he released her again. "You have no idea what you've just done! I shall have your head for this!" she yelled. Unfazed by her threats, Jester was more concerned for his nose, although the bleeding had stopped. The woman was about to speak when she looked at Jester closely. She squinted at him. "Your nose, it's…" "Broken rather nicely I'm afraid" said Jester matter of factly. The woman looked down momentarily, then into Jesters watering eyes. "I can fix that for you if you wish" she said quietly. She reached out to Jester but the troop withdrew all their swords again. The sound of steel, scraping on steel rang in the small clearing. "It's alright sergeant! I'm in no immediate danger!" said Jester. He looked at the woman and nodded. She again reached out to jester and placed both hands on either side of his face. Slowly and gently she brought her hands together at his now very painful nose. She closed her eyes in concentration. Jester looked at her and was surprised at himself. She really was beautiful. He wanted to kiss her at that moment. Suddenly she opened her eyes and seemed to look right through him. He felt an odd sensation in his face, almost a numbness of sorts. He stared into her eyes. She almost smiled back at him as if having read his thoughts of kissing her, then released her hold of him and stepped back. "It is done" she proclaimed. Jester instinctively touched his nose. In amazement, he felt his nose arrow straight again, his eyes no longer watering, no pain anymore. He was about to thank her when she bolted from the clearing, back the way they had come from the inferno of the grass!

Jester gave chase. She was amazingly fast on her feet! He was unable to gain on her at all. He could hear the men on horseback crashing through the trees to try and stop her. Fully half of them getting tangled or clothes lined on low heavy branches! She ran into the middle of the now burnt clearing just as the great dragon, powerful rear legs far forward, wings raised to spill the air beneath them, touched down. The sunlight glinted off its iridescent blue-green scales. The woman leapt onto its neck and both rose skyward! Several of the archers armed their long bows and took rapid aim! "Hold fast!" yelled Jester. Even a well placed bolt from a longbow would just shatter harmlessly against an adult dragons armoured scales, besides, he didn't want the woman hurt! He somehow knew they would cross paths again. He ordered the men to return to the castle just beyond the trees. He had some unfinished business in the still smoking grass. As the last of his men left, he strode to the center of the charred clearing and found the 'loaf'. He picked it up. Still very warm to the touch, it was seemingly just a rock, although it was much heavier than he expected of its size. He noticed a broad, flat rock face with some kind of writing just visible in the earth. He brushed some of the dirt away. It was quite large but mostly buried beneath the ground. The lettering was carved into the rock face. He could not read the words on it, perhaps some ancient writing of sorts. He made note if its location and would return another time. With the stone in hand, he too, returned to the castle.

Chapter Three

(Jester meets Zara)

Jester had placed the heavy stone on the center of the great-room's huge wooden table. He sat with his legs crossed and heels on the edge of the table at one end and regarded the stone. What was so special about this…..simple stone? He thought of the beautiful stranger he'd met. What did she mean I've ruined it all? Clearly he had interrupted some kind of ritual perhaps. At length, he got up and rolled the stone along the table top. It had a curious wobble to it. It's center of gravity clearly not normal for its size and shape. He rolled the stone back the other way and let go. It not only kept rolling, but seemed to actually speed up a little on its own! He managed to catch the stone just before it disappeared off the end of the table. He tried another experiment with the stone. He placed it in the center of the table again, then went to one end and with some effort, lifted the tables end. He expected the stone to roll away from him; instead it began to roll towards him! Uphill! As the stone accelerated up the incline, Jester dropped the table and was just able to duck as the stone shot over him and crashed onto the floor where it rolled hard into the far wall. It spun round several times and began another roll to wards him. He rolled quickly and again the stone hurtled past and into the great hearth of the fireplace where it hit hard, shedding bits of stone. It spun wildly, and again Jester was just able to avoid being struck! The stone was obviously possessed! He stood quickly and leapt onto the table top just as the possessed stone made yet another high speed roll down the room's length and into the heavy door at one end, causing splinters to fly and shedding a few more crumbs of stone in the process. Jester spied his prized cave bear rug on the wall next to the hearth. Its head intact with gleaming white teeth barred! He ran over to the wall and grabbed the heavy rug from its mounts. The stone charged again, Jester held the great rug like a bull fighter and threw it over the stone, tackling it. The rug and Jester managed to contain the wild stone momentarily. Jester lifted the rug up like a huge bag, intending to knot it closed with the four clawed legs. The stone shook and wobbled its way down through the fur and wedged inside the rugs 'head'. He lost his grip with the sudden change in weight and dropped the bear rug to the floor. The bear charged at him. Jester managed to throw himself onto the table again, foiling the latest charge. As he stood on the table bracing for another attack, the heavy door flew open and his sergeant entered the room. His jaw dropped at what he saw! Jester was standing on the table madly waving him off. All of the large strongly made chairs were broken and laying in pieces scattered about the room. Bits of stone covered the floor. And a large brown, very fierce looking bear, charging towards him! He drew his sword and managed to side step the attacker, skilfully stabbing the beast in the back of the neck. It was pinned to the floor by the sword and couldn't move further. Jester, relief spreading from his face, got down from the table and was about to congratulate the sergeant on his 'kill'. The bear strained against the swords sharp blade. Incredibly, the head tore itself free from the skewered body and chased both Jester and the sergeant back onto the table top. One of the table legs cracked. It was a table for planning, and eating at. Not for two heavy grown men to jump on! The head hit another leg of the table hard. It cracked and moved the table closer to the open doorway. Several more hits and they were almost to the doorway and potential freedom! The left rear leg broke first, causing the table to tip wildly. Booth men knelt and grabbed an edge to keep from being thrown onto the floor. Another strong impact and two more legs snapped tilting the table ramp-like towards the open doorway. Jester and his sergeant were about to jump for the steps leading downwards to the outer courtyard doors when the table took a final hit. The table top with both men clinging to it, went tobogganing down the steps to the great double doors at the bottom. Jester hung on tightly, risking a quick backwards glance at the bears head in the doorway.

The men were anxiously waiting for news of what was happening in the great-room and had gathered en-mass at the doors. Several guards were listening at the door when they suddenly exploded open! Pieces of door, Jester and the sergeant clinging to the remains of the table top and a few hapless guards crashed onto the cobblestone courtyard and skittered across its width and into the thick castle outer wall. Dazed, everyone was silent and unprepared for what happened next! The bears snarling head rolled down the last few steps into the courtyard. The men scrambled out of the way! The head came to a dizzy stop in front of a shaken Jester and sergeant. The sergeant grabbed the fearsome head with both hands. He looked at Jester who nodded. The sergeant raised the head off the ground. Jester reached inside and caught the stone, except it wasn't a stone anymore! The sergeant dropped the head in amazement! All the men stood in complete bewildered silence. A few crossed themselves quickly and glanced skyward. Jester held a wriggling baby dragon by its short tail. It made a strange 'trilling' sound and stared at Jester, un-blinking as only dragons can do.

Chapter Four

(A new baby)

What Jester didn't know is that baby dragons 'imprint' at birth. Much like goslings and ducklings imprint on their mothers upon hatching. Jester was being 'imprinted' into the little dragon's memory. He was now a dragon mom! It is a life long imprint or bond, if you will. Nothing can change an imprint once formed, except death. Jester smiled at the little dragon baby and looked over at his sergeant, who seemed uncomfortable now. He shrugged. That was that thought the sergeant. He produced a sharp dagger and offered it to Jester. "And what am I to do with that?" he asked. "Well surely sir, you're not going to keep the wretched creature?" asked the sergeant. "Well, I just can't kill it can I? Besides its kind of cute I think." Now the sergeant rolled his eyes. "You can't just keep a dragon! What happens when it's fully grown? It's not like a dog or cat sir. It's a…..dragon! They burn things like people and villages and the like."

"Yes, you're quite right sergeant. I'll finish it off, just not in front of the men." Jester said matter of fact. He rose, still holding the dragon baby at arms length. Jester wasn't sure it could make fire at that point. If it sensed its own demise, it might try to defend itself. He walked back through the shattered remains of the doors to the great-room, the little dragon still dangling by its tail. He paused before going further and turned to no one in particular. "Can this damage be repaired soon?" Jester entered the war zone that was his great-room and sat on the hearth. The beautiful table was now destroyed. Only the four legs remained and chairs broken beyond repair lay littered about the floor. This dragon baby was quite heavy he thought as he took the sergeant's dagger and held it to the dragon's belly. All Jester had to do was a simple slice and it would be the end of the dragon. The little eyes followed every move he made. Strange, but it offered no resistance to being held up by its tail or the dagger by its round belly. It just kept staring at him quietly. Jester felt uncomfortable with what he must do next. He took the dragon into his bedchamber to find a piece of clothing to wrap it in. He didn't want the little one to witness its own death. Absent minded he set the dragon down on his bed while he rummaged for some clothing he could part with for a makeshift shroud of sorts. Meanwhile, the dragon baby found a feather pillow of Jesters and curled up into it. It was asleep a moment later, exhausted from the 'hatching' process. At length Jester found an old piece of cloth from a bottom drawer and turned to the dragon asleep on his pillow. He was about to grab the dragon and wrap it up when he knew in his heart he couldn't do it. For a dragon, it was almost cute, like all babies born to this world. Puppies, kittens, bear cubs, foals, even piglets! Ok, and baby dragons too! He let it sleep, tossing the cloth into the pile of clothing strewn about the room and left. He was ravenous by now and headed for the market stalls to get something substantial to eat!

He was gulping down a goblet of ale and finishing off a piece of fire roasted chicken, when he saw one of the old storytellers hobbling past him at the market. He waved the old woman over and made room for her on the stone slab he sat on. She was a big woman and sat heavily beside him, never making eye contact with Jester. She stared straight ahead and fidgeted with her bag containing items used in her storytelling. Jester got straight to the point. "Tell me madam, what do you know of young dragons? Hatchlings, to be precise." He felt her stiffen slightly beside him. There was a pause long enough that he was about to re-ask the question. "You have taken in such a creature, I know this to be true" she said almost tonelessly. "Has the beast gazed upon you yet young man?" she asked. "Well yes, id say for some time really, it finally stopped staring long enough to fall asleep" stated

Jester, a little un-nerved by the woman's up to the minute knowledge of things. The storyteller turned and looked sternly at Jester, "You have begun a journey to which there is no foreseeable end. A dragon forms a lifelong bond to those it first gazes upon. Broken by death only, the dragon is yours, and only yours. You have a great responsibility now young man". She turned away from him and looked skyward, "A dragon is a great gift to a man. You must protect it and it will protect you. It will die in your service but it has many gifts to offer those that will see!" At that, she rose up and continued on her way as if never having spoken to him. He had so many more questions to ask of her. Someone in this kingdom must know of the dragon's ways. Surely he could find such a person! If in fact they existed at all. He would make inquiries! He thought of the woman from earlier today. She would know of dragons no doubt. To be able to fly with a dragon was almost inconceivable, but he'd witnessed it with his own eyes! It was possible! He wanted to know what he'd 'ruined'. Mostly, he wanted to just kiss her. The mysterious Grey Princess! Where was she?"

Jester entered the training area just outside the main gates and found his sergeant. "Afternoon sir, quite the day so far I'd say. I take it our little friend is now resting in peace?" said the sergeant matter of factly. "Well, yes, sergeant. Resting is one way to put it. All is calm once again, back to normal, whatever that is around here." He laughed. "A creature such as a dragon would bring many untold disasters into the kingdom sir, you did the right thing. Tough little bugger though! Gave us a bit of a run for the money eh?" said the sergeant in a confidential tone. Jester admired his sergeant, always a simple no-nonsense approach to things. The men respected him and worked hard to keep favour with him. He was lucky to have such a good man as his friend and protector when the situation was unfavourable. "Sergeant, I want you to send out scouts to find our mysterious lady friend from earlier today. I wish to speak with her further as to the events we encountered in the clearing. Keep it subtle mind you. I don't want news of this reaching her before I do. Oh, and round me up someone who knows more about dragons than we do. Someone creditable. Someone who really knows the dragon way, if you will." "Certainly sir, I have a few men in mind to do the scouting, very subtle, I assure you." The sergeant winked at Jester.

Jester entered his bed chamber expecting to see the little dragon still asleep on a pillow, but it was gone! The window was open from early this morning. It was a vertical drop of nearly one hundred feet to the ground. He doubted the dragon could fly yet, no tiny body at the base of the wall….hmmmm…..where would you go if you were a hatchling dragon? Jester suddenly ran for the larder.

The food was kept in a cold room to keep it from spoiling, right next to the cooking room. The small door was ajar. He yanked hard on the handle. The door swung open and his jaw went slack! Buried within the ribcage of a freshly butchered deer, was the baby dragon! It was barely able to move, its belly very round and firm looking. Jester pulled the little one out from the remains of his next feast and held it up to him. It stared at him quizzically without blinking. Dragons have only a single 'eyelid' to the outside edge of the eyes that closes sideways when they sleep. When awake, they have an unsettling gaze to the observer. Usually their last, before they are burnt to ashes. Jester carried the pot-bellied creature back out to the greatroom and placed it on the hearth where he sat beside it. It crawled onto his lap immediately and made that strange 'trilling' sound. Jester stared for a moment then made a low whistle like one of the forest birds. The dragons head tilted sideways as if listening intently. He made the bird call a second time. The hatchling tilted its head the other way and 'trilled' back. Jester laughed out loud at this and placed his index finger on its forehead. The little dragon rubbed against his finger like a friendly cat might do. "You're certainly a cheery little thing." He said to the little dragon. At that, he picked up the dragon and held it close to his face for the first time. The dragon baby stared back, then yawned, displaying tiny needle like teeth. Just like the monster from this morning's adventure but in scale

with its small size. "Remind me not to let you bite, my
little friend." He was beginning to have doubts about his
keeping the dragon baby. It wont stay little forever. He
stood up and carried the dragon against his shoulder as if
it were a small child, to the bedchamber. He placed it on
the bed and lay down for a nap. It had been a big day so
far. The dragon crawled up beside him and gently pushed
its muzzle under his arm. He raised his arm slightly and
the dragon curled up against the inside of his elbow, tail
over its muzzle and closed its eyes. Jester, although ready
for sleep, could not. Visions of the grey princess and the
huge adult dragon made that impossible.

Jester awoke with a start. Someone was urgently
pounding on the bedchamber door! He carefully sat
up, trying not to disturb the sleeping dragon at his side.
He rose and opened the door a crack. "Just a moment
sergeant, ill be right out." Quickly he covered the
hatchling with a corner of his top sheet and left the room,
taking care to close the door behind him. "Now, what
is it sergeant?" he asked. "Well, sir, one of my scouts has
returned with news of the mysterious woman we met
earlier. She is, well sir, she is known as the 'Grey Princess'
sir. Not evil, but not what you'd call sweet. She lives in a
rather run down manor house not a days ride from here
sir. She keeps to herself, no visitors, well except her father."
"Her father is who"? asked Jester. "None other than, Lord

Dunvegan sir!" said the sergeant, a little uneasily. "Lord
Dunvegan's daughter? I had no idea he had a daughter,
or a wife for that matter. He has a rather poor reputation
with most everyone in the kingdom. Are you absolutely
sure of this?" queried Jester. "Yes sir, my scouts a good
one. I believe what he tells me." said the sergeant. "Lord
Dunvegan was a great magician once. Then there was
the business of the Kings eldest son, wanting to learn the
magic ways. Found dead one day in the lands Dunvegan
owned. He fell out of favour with everyone. Is his wife
still with him?" "Yes sir, but she's infirm, sickly and unable
to care for herself. Apparently Dunvegan has a nurse
living in his meagre home looking after her. The rumours
are he himself caused the infirmness with a spell gone
wrong. A misinterpretation from an ancient book some
say. That kind of magic is irreversible." said the sergeant
uncomfortably. The sergeant was a man with both feet
solidly planted in reality. Things magical, unreal, and
others like dragons, left him uncomfortable, though
he dealt with those issues regularly in the course of his
duties. Today was a good example, but surely as the sun
rises, not the last. Jester met the sergeant's steady gaze and
said, "Tomorrow I'm paying the Grey Princess a surprise
visit." "I'll have the men and horses ready at sun up sir."
"Sergeant, you and the men will wait here for my return.
This is to be a private matter, if you will." said Jester.
"Very well sir, do watch your back though. If I may add,

her dragon friend may not fancy a visit from you at all. A rescue will take some time to reach you." The sergeant winked at Jester, and left the room. Jester smiled. As he crossed the greatroom floor he could smell smoke. It was coming from his bedchamber!

He burst into the room to find the little dragon on the center of the bed making smoke rings, then snapping happily at them! Its wings fluttered excitedly and were fanning the rings, into a light haze. Just as he was about to scold the dragon, another pounding came at the greatroom door. "You behave!" he said to the dragon baby. "Please don't burn the bed, I beg you!" he laughed and closed the door as another smoke ring came forth. Jester opened the greatroom door and there stood the old storyteller woman, with the sergeant looking rather apologetic right behind her. "Your dragon expert, sir. I was told…" Jester cut him off with a finger across his throat gesture. "Please do come in. Make yourselves comfortable." said Jester. The greatroom was pretty much the way it was after the 'bear' attack earlier. The hearth was the only place one could sit without resorting to the floor itself. The old woman made her way past the ruined furnishings to the hearth and sat down with some effort. Jester and the sergeant sat cross legged on the floor, much like two children at story time.

"The sergeant was kind enough to bring me here. Again, more dragon talk?" Jester cleared his throat and coughed, "Well yes, I wish to learn more of their ways..." Jester never finished his sentence. Behind him came a huge 'woof' sound. The sound a large fire would make if suddenly ignited! The bedchamber door blew open from the fireball inside the room. The little dragon ran straight to Jester and crawled into his arms, its wings flapping excitedly. Luckily the fire ball blew itself out upon the door blowing open. The heavy grey smoke was another matter. It filled the room's upper third and wafted slowly out the open windows. The sergeant looked at Jester and with a smile said "I take it my dagger has a poor aim sir." They both laughed, but the old woman was not amused. She looked at Jester sternly. "You have your hands full, mark my words. The dragon's way is not suited to living with men. They have needs far different from ours.

Tell me exactly how you have come to be in possession of this creature. Leave no detail out!" she commanded. Jester and the sergeant retold their tale of the morning's adventure as carefully and accurately as possible. When they finished, the old woman sat quietly regarding them both. She gestured to the sleeping dragon in Jester's lap. "This is a puzzle. She has bonded to you, that's obvious, but she exhibits few traits shared by many dragons. You sir, are its mother and protector, for now.

When she grows up, it will be you who is protected by her." she said sternly. "If I might interrupt, you called her a she. I…I mean she's a her, a female?" Jester asked. "Yes it's a she dragon. They are larger and more powerful than the males. Her wings are just forward of her front legs, the males slightly behind. Her tail, as it grows longer, will have a split tip that faces forwards, the males face rearwards. Make no mistake, dragons are extremely clever beings. Most have properties about them few understand. It is written on the large dragon-stones. It is told, there are three in this kingdom. Two of them are as yet unfound. The one I know of is in Lord Dunvegan's land, near his residence. The stones tell of the dragon's powers, and can be used to summon them by a dragon master. It is said the dragon stones were placed by the dragons themselves many years before we ever inhabited the world. Only a dragon master can read and use the stones as they were meant to be. There are others who know more about those things than I." the old woman trailed off, she seemed suddenly tired. "I can tell you this, dragon masters are not made, they are born. Sometimes many years will pass before the next one realizes his or her abilities. It's been a very long time since the kingdom has had a dragon master. The dragon's themselves must also approve of the individual before the transformation is complete. It's a matter of the heart, both human and dragon. True bonds such as these are very rare and do not happen easily." She paused, then looked down at the floor. It seemed she was searching for more to add to her explanations, but then stood to leave. Jester had more questions than answers but that would have to do for now. "You'll know where to find me if I can be of further service sir." said the sergeant. He quietly escorted the woman out.

Jester carried the sleepy dragon back to the bedchamber and placed her on the bed. He laid down himself. He was ready for sleep now. Tomorrow would be another long day. He needed a name for the dragon. A female name......suddenly it came to him. His mother wanted a sister for him when he was much younger but it never came to be. She was to be named Zara. Well, Zara it is! He fell asleep with a faint smile on his face. Zara was ahead of him. She lay on her back behind Jester and slept soundly, twitching at times to her Zara dreams.

Chapter Five

(A love interest blooms)

The next day dawned with a dark threatening sky. Jester dressed himself while Zara played dragon games with the bedding. She was attacking the very dangerous pillow creatures in turn. Her little wings flapping wildly, Zara pounced on Jesters, then the spare, and finally her 'adopted' pillow! "You're truly a fearsome beast Zara. This poor bed will never be safe!" laughed Jester. "You're now in charge of the bedchamber until my return. Be good, well, as much as you can be good! Please don't burn the bedchamber." he said. He closed the door to the chamber and headed to the stables. Zara ran to the other side of the door and 'trilled' in protest at being left behind. Jester had thought of bringing Zara along for the trip but thought better of it. The Grey Princess may want Zara returned, and he wasn't sure he would part with her now. He left through the hidden doorway in the rear of the courtyard. A rider and horse could just fit through the opening. As he rounded the castle's Eastern wall, the forest path lay ahead. He was about to ride off when he heard a shriller more panicked version of Zara's 'trilling' sound. He looked back at the castle wall in time to see Zara launch herself from the still open window of the bedchamber. His mouth open in stunned amazement, Jester witnessed little Zara open her wings as wide as she could and pitch headlong, down nearly one hundred feet of vertical stone wall! Just as certain death would come at the end of the fall, Zara managed to pull upwards at the last moment and rocketed past Jester and the startled horse. At a speed near that of a bolt from a longbow, Zara hit the trees and crashed down through the many branches. She landed hard on the path and tumbled several more times till coming to a stop in a cloud of dust, pine needles, and a few shredded leaves! Jester raced his horse to the crash scene and dismounted quickly. He knelt and picked up a motionless Zara. Surely broken from one end to the other by such fall! How could he have been so blind as to leave the window open? Suddenly he felt a tremble in the little body. Zara's eyes opened and she 'trilled' in delight. Jester could not believe how tough the little dragon was. Totally fearless as well! She seemed no worse for wear than when he left her just moments before this. He held her close for a moment, and then mounted his horse, placing a wide eyed Zara before him on the saddle. They rode quietly for the whole morning. By now, the forest had thinned out, revealing a weathered, rocky landscape with pockets of dense brush. Age worn rocks, some covered in splotches of lichen that had stood there for eons. The pathway was much more open and wound around the rock outcroppings, becoming slightly steeper from every mile onwards. The wind had picked up now as well. Zara liked to keep her nose into the wind, like a boat anchored off shore. Presently, they arrived at a crossroads. This one was unusual in that there was no highway house. Most crossroads offered an inn and brew house to wayward travellers. None such existed here. The land seemed even more desolate now with the sombre sky. Rain would likely follow. Suddenly, Zara jumped from the horse and waddled off to the side of the path. Jester was surprised when a large dark puddle formed behind the little dragon. At length, she finished her business and 'trilled' to get up on the horse with Jester again. Jester knew they were close. He could faintly smell smoke, likely from a warm hearth not far from where they were. Moments later, they came to a rise in the path and could see the run-down manor house in the distance. Once a strong and imposing house, it had been left to the elements, neglected for years. The chimneys at either end were partly toppled, as was the outer gates and guard walls. As they neared the structure, Jester noticed the courtyard in front to be neatly maintained as well as the main entrance to the old stone house. He dismounted and

simply put Zara in the large inside pocket of his cloak.
He tied the horse to a weathered old railing at the foot
of the wide steps leading to the large outer door. He felt
he was being watched, but it seemed no one was home.
He rapped on the iron door knock and waited. Zara
fidgeted inside the dark warm pocked of Jesters cloak.
He was surprised when the door opened a moment later.
A woman near his age answered the door. "Please state
your business here." she requested politely. "I am Jes…"
"Come in, please. I know who you are." she cut Jester off.
He entered a large open greatroom, fully the center of
the house. Curved stairs led up to a second floor at either
end. It was warm and surprisingly clean. "I am Shandahr,
what brings you here on such a day sir?" She was an exotic
looking woman, a real beauty. "I have come to speak
with the lady of the house. Is she here?" he asked. "She is
out on the property at this time. I am her sister. You can
state your business with me." she said, her tone was just
slightly prying. "I had no idea Lord Dunvegan had two
daughters. I see beauty runs in the family." Jester bowed
deeply, subtly holding Zara from tipping out of his large
pocket. "I believe I ran across her just yesterday, in the
forest next to my castle. A very 'warm' reception if you
understand me." Jester said plainly. He looked in her eyes
to see any spark of recognition. Her eyes gave no sign but
seemed guarded to him. "Tell me Shandahr, is your sister
known as 'The Grey Princess'? I wish very much to speak

with her if I may." asked Jester. Shandahr laughed at that. "She is known by that title in certain places, yes. She never wears anything with any color in it. Only shades of grey. She's done that since childhood. If she was dressed in a colour, a rash would form on her skin. It would make her ill, until the coloured clothing was removed. Our father said it was a sign of something special about her, something as yet unknown." said Shandahr. A brilliant flash of lightening lit the room up suddenly, followed by a rolling thunder crash! Both Shandahr and Jester startled! Jester's horse pulled heavily on the old railing mount and it broke loose. The rider less horse leaving, at a full gallop, across the field towards the path home. Jester dashed to the doorway and reached the steps in time to see the horse vanish from sight. The rain began in earnest now. Water collected in the spaces between the courtyard cobblestones. Shandahr reappeared at the doorway. "Will it return soon?" she asked. "Yes, just before darkness falls on the other side of the Eastern forest!" Jester said. "I'm sorry for that. You will find my sister near the stone hill behind us." stated Shandahr. "Thank you for that, ill go immediately!" said Jester. He bowed again to the sister; Zara tumbled over in the pocket of the cloak and 'trilled' in protest. Shandahr's eyes widened. She knew that sound and what creature it came from. She said nothing. Jester looked skyward into the rain and clouds. He made his way behind the old manor house and out through a small gate onto a well worn path leading up the stone hill Shandahr had spoken of.

By the time Jester and the now awake Zara had reached the base of the massive hill it was nearly dark. The rain had let up slightly and the overcast sky allowed a glimpse of moonlight from time to time. Jester was able to continue in the near darkness. He thought he could see a shadowy figure up ahead, barely visible in the inky black terrain of the now featureless hill. The figure darted in and out of the rock outcroppings, but continued upwards at a steady rate. Zara was now tucked into his nearly soaked tunic. The wind whipped water off the ends of his cloak and tugged at him as he climbed upwards. Ahead, the other figure paused, as if to check his progress on the hillside. Jester was steadily gaining on the other. He guessed they would reach the top at about the same time. Zara could sense Jesters urgency and quickening of the pace. She peeked out from his tunic and could see the shadow like figure just ahead now. Zara knew it was a woman by the lightness of stride. She was maybe twenty feet ahead of them when she stopped and turned to face them. Jester came to an abrupt halt. He carefully lowered the squirming Zara to the wet ground at his feet. The figure before them slowly raised both arms upwards and allowed the hooded cloak to fall to the ground revealing the familiar simple grey dress. The moonlight returned, revealing her dark beauty again. She struck Jester as even more beautiful on this wild wet hilltop. She walked to him. Zara 'trilled' and rubbed against her leg, cat like. Jester wanted to speak but could not. Her eyes held his. Gently, she took Jesters left hand and placed it on her right cheek, holding it in place. He could clearly feel her pulse through his hand. It was fast like his own. This was not at all what he had expected their next meeting to be like. Her eyes shone brightly in the moons light, holding his gaze completely. She stepped close and leaned forward slightly and kissed him full on the lips! Her other hand now behind his head to complete the embrace, this was a kiss of all kisses! It was even better than he could have imagined. Zara let out a faint 'trill' as she watched. Suddenly a gigantic bolt of lightning lit them up with its stark bluish light! The bolt split directly over them and incinerated a huge circle around them. The accompanying thunder was deafening. Jester broke off the kiss and stepped back slightly. He was about to speak. The woman placed a finger on his lips. She finally spoke. Loudly over the thunder, she told him "Where the lightening has touched earth, nothing will ever grow in this circle for a hundred years! This circle is your marker. Remember it always, for one day it will surely save your lives! A frightened Zara ran up his leg and into his tunic at the heavy sound of the thunder. Jester glanced at Zara inside his tunic. When he looked up, the Grey Princess was gone. Vanished.

Chapter Six

(A surprise)

He descended the hill towards home. The rain came in torrents. Zara was cold and wet too, although she did get some warmth from Jester's chest. After what seemed like an eternity of mud and wet, Jester and Zara arrived at the castle's front entry. The moat was alive with the rain pelting the dark water. The rain danced beneath his wet boots as he crossed the heavy wooden bridge. The massive iron chains used to raise the bridge, dribbled streams of water from the blackened links onto the bridge deck. Finally they were at the main gate. The guards nowhere to be seen on a night like this. He wasn't angered by that, only a fool with a small dragon would be out walking on a night like this. Putting his shoulder against the gate itself, Jester touched the old and time worn spring lever and pulled hard on the bronze ring on its end. The gate mechanism had no lock, but instead, relied upon the force of pull required to release the iron bolt. Too light a pull, or too heavy, the gate would fail to open. It took practice to do it correctly. After three attempts, a trap door in the bridge would drop the 'victim' into the moat well below. The trap door had been disabled after a few weeks of dunking by Jester and guards alike. The heavy gate withdrew upwards into the great stone battlements looming high above them. The promise of a warming fire and a much needed drink lay a few more sodden steps away.

Jester and a happily 'trilling' Zara entered the greatroom and stood in complete and utter amazement… the room was aglow with a warm inviting fire set in the hearth. All the chairs and the main table had been replaced, and the stone floor swept clean of the debris from earlier. But what stopped them in their tracks was a large oblong box beautifully wrapped as a gift in the middle of the room! Suddenly little Zara ran to the gift 'trilling' excitedly! She appeared to yawn, but instead sent several smoke rings into the air! Jester laughed and joined Zara on the floor beside the gift. There was a card under the carefully hand tied bow in the center. Jester removed the card and opened it. The writing simply said, 'The Next Step'. He noticed the ink was still damp on the e and p. He quickly scanned the room. It was only he and a very excited little dragon in the room. Zara was already pulling at the ribbon and lace that made up the fancy bow! Finally

the dragon's might won out over the ribbon and off flew
the bow. Carefully, they un-wrapped the gift. It was a well
made wooden box with four hinged panels that appeared
to open outwards from the center. Jester lifted the panel
nearest him. Part of a metal crest of some kind shone
from within. Zara was beside herself with the anticipation
and scrabbled open a second panel. They both paused at
the sight of a cross piece of highly polished metal shining
brightly. Neither he nor Zara had noticed the room itself
was much brighter as well. Zara finally opened the last
two panels of the box. The room brightened further than
before. Gleaming metal, polished like nothing he'd ever
seen before, shone brightly. Zara backed up a little and
'trilled' at Jester. He reached into the box and removed
the most beautiful sword he'd ever laid eyes on! Its curves
were like nothing ever seen before. It's light, radiant, as
if coming from inside the very metal itself! Jester did
not recognize the crest on the hilt. He held the sword
before him, its blade pointing upwards toward the high
ceiling. What Jester and Zara didn't see was their shadows
on the wall behind them. As Jester held the sword and
Zara looked on, their shadows were something different
entirely! Jesters shadow was a warrior holding the sword
as if to strike an enemy. The Zara shadow was a fully
grown dragon with powerful wings raised as if to take
flight. Its jaws, open wide, revealing many large pointed
teeth! Jester placed the beautiful sword back in the box

and carefully closed the four panels. The room darkened noticeably as the last panel was shut. The warm glow from the fire provided the only light to the room. Jester finally stood and scooped Zara off the floor and sat with the little dragon before the warm fire. Zara was asleep in no time at all. Her first adventure with Jester. They rested close to the fire, he was almost dry now. 'The next step', what did that mean? He was lost in is thoughts for awhile, and yawned hugely. He got up and carefully took Zara to bed. The rain continued and the distant thunder rumbled. He was laying there thinking again of the Grey Princess. That kiss was amazing! He hoped there would be another chance to meet with her, perhaps without dragons and lightning bolts. Just a moment, without any, distraction. He fell asleep with dreams of her, great dragons, Zara, and more lightning bolts.....

He awoke with banging on the bedchamber door. "Yes, what is it!" he called out. It was the sergeant as usual. "Just checking on you sir, the men noticed your horse had returned, well, ah, empty handed so to speak. Everything alright then?" "Yes, it was a lovely walk from the highlands" Jester said sarcastically. "Give me a moment sergeant, ill be out shortly." Jester got dressed and came out to the greatroom. The sergeant was admiring the wooden box on the new table. "A bit of shopping sir?" he said, still looking at the box. "I was about to ask you the same question." said Jester. The sergeant looked at Jester with eyebrows raised. "It was here when I arrived late last night. A note proclaimed it to be 'the next step'." The sergeant merely said "It?" Jester opened the box and removed the beautiful shining sword and placed it on the table next to the surprised sergeant. "Very impressive! I don't believe I've seen one anything like this before. The metal isn't one I know. What crest is it?" "I'm not sure, two dragons side by side above a chain mail gloved hand, female looking I'd say, I've never seen it before." stated Jester. The sergeant leaned closer to the crest and squinted slightly. "I can see the two dragons are not quite the same either sir. Unusually detailed, for a crest. Perhaps one of the engravers at the armoury could tell us more." said the sergeant, still closely examining the sword. "Strange." he said to Jester with out looking away from the sword. "There is no apparent mechanical connection to either the hilt guard or the actual handle from the blade as is normal practice. It appears to be of a single piece of this strange metal. Nothing like this workmanship in the kingdom sir, I'd know if there was." stated the sergeant. Yet another mystery, thought Jester. "Sergeant, who exactly delivered this gift to the greatroom yesterday, and lit the warming fire?" asked Jester directly. "Sir, no one to my knowledge entered this room other then the men with the new table and chairs, plus the sweeps to tidy the mess from the 'little ones' escapades of the day before." said the sergeant simply. "Surely someone noticed such a beautiful gift being placed in this room!" said Jester, just slightly exasperated at this. The sergeant picked up on Jester's tone and said to him "Sir, I'll question the men, the guards in particular, and get to the bottom of this. I assure you, if any one saw anything, ill find out about it!" At that, he left the greatroom, and headed straight to the barracks. He was as keen as Jester to find the gifter! He would also stop at the armoury and chat with the chief engraver as well. That sword was amazing, in that it appears to be a single unified piece of metal he'd never seen before. The armoury was one of the best in the kingdom, Jester's new sword did not compare to anything he had ever seen built before. He would have it copied if at all possible. That was certain.

The sergeant and Jester knew each other all to well. They were childhood friends, although Jester was younger, they struck up a friendship that remains to this day. It would be 20 years this spring they had goofed about as kids with wooden practice swords and imaginary foes. They would all be vanquished with sword play and a little imagination from the two. He was in his 30th year of life, Jester was 26. Jester had the advantage of fearlessness, and no apparent thinking before his actions. He just did what the moment required. Even now, a nod or rolling of eyes was a signal to the other that made a real connection between them. The sergeant loved his ranking and carried out his orders to the letter as Jester commanded. It was play for real now. This was one of those times he needed answers for his friend. He didn't like mysteries. There were many mysteries in this life, and the more he could solve, the better! Most were grounded in facts, however some remained elusive. Like Zara, a hatchling dragon. How could Jester fall in love with the unknown, the unproven? He felt it would make a horrendous pet, no matter how friendly it was. Just imagine twenty tons of dragon wanting to play. How do you scold it for burning a village? Where would it go and do its business? The orderliness of the castle would decline into appalling conditions with a dragon on the property. Things of magic were not his favourite dealings. It left one unsure of what was real or not. However, this was the sergeant's life now, take it or leave it, he could not imagine life without his friend!

The day dawned bright and sunny. Jester and Zara played games only they could understand. The men as always were itching to go on the next adventure as ordered. The sergeant, in particular. One day Jester had practiced with the new sword. It was light and very well balanced! He learned its weight and its balance carefully. It was a sword like none other. It was almost an extension of his arm, maybe his very thoughts. It seemed to almost anticipate his desire and make the opponent loose their will to fight. Before long, his slightly bent sword from earlier was now in the closet as was most other short term loves of everything battle oriented. This sword was somehow different. He came to realize, that it held a sort of residual magic. It was light weight but hit with the power of a broadsword. More than a few times it cut completely through a broadsword wielding opponent's sword, ending the match! After weeks of practice the sword showed none of the usual signs of wear. In fact, not a single mark was left on the sword. It was as new as the first time he ever held it back on that rain soaked night when he and Zara discovered the gift wrapped box in the greatroom. The armoury had built a new sheath for the sword from the finest materials at hand. Jester carried the sword at his belt always. Zara was never far from his side either. She accompanied Jester daily. Chasing all manner of bugs, birds and small mammals. Some ended up incinerated to mere ashes, others escaped to play another day. It was the dragon way. Zara was very inquisitive. She was determined to explore the realm she lived in thoroughly. This did create problems though. The market vendors were dismayed at the losses of poultry, impromptu cooking and all manner of food thefts. Jester finally had to keep Zara from running loose in the courtyard. She had the run of the castle interior but out doors she was closely watched.

The sergeant knocked on Jester's door. "Sir, I have some people to look at the sword if you're willing." The sergeant had brought the chief armourer, the engraver and one of the craftsmen who built the swords used by his own troop. Jester removed the sword from its box and placed the sword on the greatroom table. The group from the armoury went over the sword very carefully. Squinting, touching, wielding and puzzling. Zara watched from her perch on Jesters shoulder. She liked to be close to him when not involved in Zara things, like eating and testing her fire breathing abilities. At length, the chief armourer whispered into the sergeant's ear. The sergeant cleared his throat and said, "Sir, it is for certain the sword is a single piece of metal. No screws, bolts or any other connection between the hilt, guard or blade. Secondly, the metal is unknown. Nothing we have can match the strength or quality of this sword, anywhere in the kingdom." The engraver coughed and added, "Sir, if I may speak freely," Jester nodded. "The crest is most interesting sir. It depicts two female dragons facing each other as if to square off in a battle of sorts. Both dragons are anatomically correct and of different breeds sir. Even the number of scales is correct and different for each dragon profile. Absolutely amazing sir, it's an art we do not share with the maker of this sword. The chain mail hand is most definitely a woman's. A most unusual addition, I might add sir. The detail is impressive as to its accuracy. Frankly, I've never seen anything like it, ever." The engraver paused and regarded the sword. "Crests are a simplistic representation of a family usually. This one depicts the, well, ah, the power of a woman, sir." stammered the engraver. Jester was intrigued by this. His first thought was of the Grey Princess. It so felt like her, but he had no real proof. Even if he did, what did it matter, besides perhaps getting more swords of this rare quality. Jester knew in his heart, the sword was a one time build. It was spectacularly singular in its make up. It had a special purpose, 'the next step' as yet unknown…

Chapter Seven

(Hotdogs and a party!)

It was almost midday when Jester awoke from a very fitful sleep. He'd been dreaming of the Grey Princess. Zara was rolled up in the bedding as usual, leaving only a small corner of blanket for Jester to cover himself with. He was hungry and dressed quickly. He then grabbed hold of the sheet Zara was rolled up in and lifted it high above the bed. Zara was unwound in the sheet very quickly! At the last second she bit into the sheet before falling free to the bed itself. She just hung there, slowly turning as the last of the blanket straightened out from its windings. Her legs hung loosely by her side, and her tail straight. Jester laughed and shook the blanket to dislodge her. Instead, Zara's needle like teeth ripped a large strip of the blanket at a diagonal, allowing her to gently reach the bed. She released the torn end and staggered slightly dizzy from the unwinding to the edge of the bed in front of Jester. He placed his index finger to

Zara's muzzle and she rubbed against it. It was a friendly dragon greeting of sorts, he guessed. This ritual was carried out most every morning. Now it was time to eat, thought Jester.

With Zara close to his feet, he made his way among the food vendors in the courtyard. It all looked and smelled so good. He felt like he hadn't eaten in days. He kept a wary eye on Zara. She had no manners at all. If there was something she fancied eating, she would either jump or climb the vendors cart and grab it and start eating there and then. The perplexed vendor, unsure on how best to remove Zara, and food from the cart. Sometimes she would hiss with open jaws at anyone brave enough to attempt picking her up from their cart! A new vendor to the courtyard offered a lean sausage of some kind, wrapped in a soft white bun. It smelled good with the raw onion, a tomato sauce, and some finely chopped cucumber mixed with dill weed. Jester bought five of them and he and Zara returned to the castle greatroom to eat. Jester placed Zara at one end of the table on a chair with a large block of wood so she could see across the table top, Jester sat at the other end with all the food from the vendor. He held the first sausage in the bun and took a huge bite. As he swallowed it stuck in the back of his throat. He coughed strongly, and the partly chewed food shot across the table towards Zara. Her little eyes

were quick, and her reactions quicker still! She caught
the food in her mouth with an audible snap, it was gone!
Jester wasn't sure he believed his eyes or not. He carefully
broke a piece of sausage and bun off with his hands. Zara
looked on as if mesmerized by the action. Her unblinking
gaze following every tiny move he made with his hands.
He placed another chunk in his mouth. Suddenly he hit
both of his cheeks with closed fists and shot the sausage
and bun towards Zara. In a single heartbeat Zara caught
the food with a lightening fast 'snap' of her jaws. The
food had vanished! She swallowed it whole, no chewing
at all. Jester finished the first one in this way. He un-
wrapped the second one and broke it into three more or
less equal pieces. This time he tossed them at Zara in rapid
succession. One, two, three! The first was still in the air
as the last was tossed. Zara's mouth opened three times.
In three snaps, all the food had disappeared well before
hitting the table top. This little dragon was good! Zara was
becoming very excited by this new game. She had very
subtly left her chair and was balanced on the top edge of
the table now. Jester did the same with the next sausage
and bun. However this time, he added to Zara's level of
difficulty by throwing all three pieces at once, high above
the table! Zara expertly manuevered herself on the table
top and caught all three pieces of sausage and bun. The
last one however was caught as she fell off the table, her
entire focus on the food, not her position on the table.

With a thump, she hit the floor, swallowed and let loose with a small fireball towards Jester. His left shoulder was lightly ablaze and he beat at it with his cloth place mat. A second small fire ball shot out of the happy dragon again and set his right sleeve on fire! Jester managed to snuff it out quickly! There came a pounding at the door again. The sergeant entered the room just in time for Jester's shoulder and arm to re-ignite! Dragon fire is a persistent thing! Both Jester and the sergeant managed to put out the fire again. Dragons can control the type and the intensity of their fire at will. Zara was just playing and kept it low key. Jester was amazed at how such a little dragon could do what she had done. By the time the fires were out so were the two remaining sausages and buns. She had eaten all but one bite. She had saved that for him. He picked her up and hugged her. As he set her down on the table, his right forearm re-ignited! He made a promise to himself not to try this at bed time. Jester suddenly realized he had not eaten any of the treats he had just thrown to Zara! He reached over the table and ate the piece Zara had left for him. She had actually shared with him! That was amazing. The little dragon had eaten all five of the sausage and buns he had brought with them. A big appetite for a little one! The sergeant just shook his head with that.

Jester was always the animal lover and protector. Since he was a child, all manner of cats and dogs befriended him and vice versa! It was just the way things were with him. Even his nickname,' Jester' was from his constant dry humour. He found something funny about most things. He liked to laugh, even at himself. It was a rare trait among men. He was very serious when he needed to be though, but his smile was never far away. Even after both his parents had died in the 'Great War', Jester had kept his innate sense of humour. It was his way, and likely always would be. He had been left a title, and lands at their passing. His father knew the king well, and Jester had been readily accepted as a knight protectorate in the kingdom of Tyde. He even had a royal seal which was used in all correspondence he had. His sergeant and every man in his troop thought very highly of him. He was easy going and fair to a fault. He would ask nothing of any man he was not prepared himself to carry out.

The sergeant had brought news of lord Dunvegan. Apparently his wife had died a day ago. There was to be a funeral in two days time and Jester and an entourage were invited to pay their last respects. Jester told the sergeant to select an honour guard to accompany him and the sergeant to Dunvegan's home the following day. He had an ulterior motive in that he may see the Grey Princess again. Hopefully without adult dragons or lightning bolts!

The sergeant was now very busy. All the tack for the horses needed to be cleaned and oiled, as did the men's armour and boots. Jester was fastidious that the troop and any honour guard look their very best! Jester followed the sergeant out as far as the courtyard and got three more of the sausages with buns. He ate them almost as fast as Zara had, but unlike the dragon, he chewed each piece before swallowing. They were very good he thought, no wonder Zara liked them so much! Easy to eat, no mess and easy to carry around! Those might really catch on around the kingdom he thought. They did need a catchy name though...

Everyone in the castle was excited as tonight there was to be a great feast in honour of all the animals in the kingdom. The animals offered meats of all kinds, eggs, all manner of dairy foods, and leathers, wool for all types of clothing, and in many cases, companionship to those that kept them as pets. It included the castle cats which were unique to Jester. Rarely was a mouse or rat seen on the property. Thanks to them, disease was unusual in his lands. This was Jester's big night and he was getting ready to be the host for tonight's festivities. The cooks worked tirelessly preparing the food for the event. The maids cleaned and dusted as well as made ready the hundreds of heavy candles and wall torches to be lit in the greatroom and outdoors in the courtyard below just before sunset.

Jester and Zara napped in the bedchamber. Jester didn't want to start yawning too early in the evening. Zara would remain in the bedchamber with the window closed tightly. Everyone in his lands had been invited to the event. The castle would be overflowing with guests, food, wine, and ales. This celebration of the animals was unique to Jester's region. No other land holder had done anything like this before. Jester had invited the heads of the other lands to attend the feast and enjoy his hospitality. Most came every year and marvelled in the sheer fun everyone seemed to have. Even the animals were treated to the best food and bedding that night! He would save Zara's debut for later in the evening.

The first of the guests began arriving as the shadows were growing longer in the courtyard. More and more guests kept coming! This was going to be a wonderfully busy night for all! Zara was beside herself with excitement! She seemed to enjoy being around people. A very un-dragon like behaviour. Jester gave the nod to the staff to light the torches and many candles throughout the castle. The night of celebration had begun. Many of the repeat guests brought food items for the animals to enjoy, and then worked their way to the greatroom. The sergeant and the guards were busy getting the guests coaches and horses parked, then fed and watered. It was getting jammed in the courtyard and beyond the main gates. So many visitors!

By now most of the guests were packed into the greatroom. All manner of animals roamed the castle freely. The clean up staff would have a lot to do the next day! Jester circulated among the many guests. Some were old friends, some he had not met before tonight. Everyone was having fun. He secretly hoped the Grey Princess would show up, but not so far. Everyone was eating and drinking! The castle was usually never this busy. He always made a brief speech to the guests about how thankful everyone was for the animals in the kingdom, etc. Tonight he had planned to introduce Zara to everyone! He was, however, not completely convinced this was a great idea. Everyone might just bolt from the castle celebrations never to return with a dragon on the loose! Zara was somewhat unpredictable still, having been set ablaze himself, with her excitement with the food, it might be too risky yet. As Jester worked his way through the crowded room he noticed the wife of his stable manager. She was wearing a very bright, very yellow dress. She was a big woman and most unpleasant in her gossip of everything in the kingdom. She had few friends and many enemies! She was a most pompous woman. Jester tried to avoid her gaze but no such luck! "Sir Jester!" she exclaimed, much too forcefully to be even remotely genuine. "What a lovely 'gathering'!" she gushed. "Everyone looks so happy!" she said in a way that made you think all the happy people were just pretending. "Kisses from Jester?" she cooed, as if talking to a four year old. She turned an overly made up cheek towards him. Suddenly Jester felt a tug on his leg! It was Zara climbing up his leg! How did she escape the bedchamber? Just as he was about to land a forced and polite kiss on her cheek, Zara was perched on top of his shoulder. The woman's strong a perfume made Zara sneeze. Dragon sneezes involve a large smoke ring. Zara hissed at the woman just as she turned to face Jester! She was almost eye to snout with Zara, who was very unsettled by her odour and the garish make up she wore. The woman stared and blinked a moment. Zara stared back, jaws slightly open, showing her needle teeth as she tilted her head slightly. The woman's eyes rolled up into her head and she fainted. Jester tried to catch her but she dropped heavily to the floor. The crowd parted, open mouthed at the faint woman and more so at Jester with a dragon perched on his right shoulder. Zara flapped her wings and let out another smoke ring. It was deathly silent in the room suddenly. Several other ladies crumpled to the floor. "It's alright everyone! Nothing to fear I assure you!" boomed the sergeant's voice from behind Jester. "The little one has befriended Jester and is very tame, like a cat!" Jester turned and looked at the sergeant, who shrugged back, both palms upwards. Jester rolled his eyes at the sergeant and turned to face the crowd, now chatting again amongst themselves. "He's correct ladies and gentlemen. I'd like you all to meet Zara! The newest addition to the household! We found her, or, rather I found her in the forest awhile ago and, well, I'm,…" Jester turned back to his sergeant with a shrug. The sergeant suddenly climbed onto a chair to be seen by all in the room. "Everyone! A toast to the newest animal in the kingdom! Long live Zara!" the sergeant held up his goblet, then, drank till it was empty. The crowd of guests murmured then drank to the sergeant's toast. Zara leaned into Jester's neck and was content to ride on his shoulders the rest of the evening. Many of the guests gathering their courage came to greet Zara, who delighted in making more smoke rings. Soon the party was back to everyone having fun except the stable manager's wife. She sat near the hearth and drank much more wine to ease her 'pains'. Everything was going well again when a cat, chased by a small dog entered the greatroom. The cat hissed and spat at the terrier, which barked and continued chasing the cat. Zara was ready to play too! With a flapping of her wings she launched herself off Jester and joined the chase. The three of them caused the crowd to weave unsteadily on their feet. Parting at times, to allow the threesome passage amongst the forest of feet and legs. The cat was managing to just stay ahead of the feisty terrier. Zara was trying to keep up with both! The cat saw a break in its path and jumped upwards, landing squarely on the bosom of the stable manager's wife! Followed very closely by the unruly terrier, with Zara a heartbeat behind the dog. In what was just a single moment, all three animals crashed into the poor woman's torso, knocking her and her wine backwards into the great fireplaces archway. Thankfully the fire had not been set so far. The woman, cat, dog and dragon all rolled into the black sooty fireplace. Clouds of black soot billowed forth from the fireplace amid terrified shrieks, hissing, and growling sounds. Jester and the sergeant ran to the rescue. Amid the clouds of soot it was hard to really see who had who! The poor woman was rolled up in her own dress much like Zara in the bedding. The cat had wedged itself about six feet up the chimney, with the terrier jumping and barking wildly. Zara was on top of the now totally soot blackened woman. Her wings flapping excitedly, causing even more soot to billow out from the hearth. Jester grabbed Zara while the sergeant carefully rolled the woman out of the hearth and onto the stone floor. The sergeant desperately tried to unravel her but could not tell which end was what. The crowd made room in front of the fireplace and were laughing harder than they ever had at the perplexed sergeant attempting to unwind the huge, not so yellow dress. Suddenly the room went very quiet. Jester, having just rinsed off Zara, returned in time to see the Grey Princess wading through the now silent crowd of guests. She made her way to the blackened bundle on the floor near the hearth. The sergeant bowed, and stepped back awkwardly. The Grey Princess grabbed her cloak and swung it upwards and over the woman on the floor. In that instant, a blindingly bright flash of light lit the room for a split second! By the time the cloak had returned to her side the woman stood shakily as if nothing had ever happened. Her dress was as yellow and voluminous as before. The soot and ash were completely gone, and the hearth as tidy as before. Even the cat and the terrier sat together, as if friends. Jester approached her with an outstretched hand. She took his hand in hers. Jester nervously, but politely, kissed it and welcomed her with a wink. "So how does a lady get a drink around here?" she said to no one in particular. Jester looked pleadingly at the sergeant. "Would a nice red wine suit the lady?" asked the sergeant. "It would indeed suit." she said. By now the crowd was back in the party spirit and the room filled once again with the many conversations. A lot of them about dragons. Jester marvelled at the Grey Princess. She could take command of a party or a room of people with out any effort at all. She knew what needed to be done and having done that, it was like she was nothing special at all. Jester admired that in her. She had to be his age, or perhaps a bit older. She was always in control of things. She really didn't need a man in her life at all other than possibly for companionship. Jester found that almost irresistible, other

than her obvious beauty. She could more than look after
herself, with or without her magic. She was always politely
in control of everything around her, well, except Jester.
The Princess knew he was a wild card, hence her attraction
to him. He was not easily controlled like most men
allowed. Unlike many others, Jester acted and reacted
from his heart. A strong sense of right and wrong,
tempered with fairness. She knew Jester was beginning to
fall for her. The truth was, so was she falling for him. It
would be a 'delicate' situation for a while but she wanted
to take another step forward in their budding romance.
The sergeant returned with her wine in a massive goblet.
"My sincerest apologies my lady for the size of the goblet,
we were not able to…." she cut him off with a curtsy and a
smile. "Thank you, sergeant. It's just right. It will save me
from getting another for awhile!" She took the goblet from
the sergeant with both hands and took a long drink. Both
Jester and the sergeant looked at each other. The sergeant
turned his palms up. He left to get himself another drink.
Jester regarded the princess with out being too obvious.
Her hair was short for the times, several inches above her
shoulders. It suited her face well, and must be easy to keep
that way. She turned to him and linked her arm with his
as they began to make their way through the crowded
room. "It dries quickly too she said." Jester was speechless,
but knew she could follow his thoughts when she chose to.
"Tell me about…Zara," she said, as if asking about an

Aunt of his. "Zara! Of course! Hahah!" His laugh was a
bit manic sounding, even to Jester. "Well, why don't you
see for yourself?" said Jester, a bit uncomfortable with this.
He guided the princess to the very busy food preparation
area in the castle cooking room. On the huge pot holder,
above the washing table, was Zara. She 'trilled' in delight
and jumped to Jester's shoulder. The Princess held out a
many ringed finger and Zara rubbed against it like she did
for Jester. It was then he noticed on one of her rings, the
same crest as his sword displayed. He made a mental note
to ask her about the crest. "She is very relaxed with so
many people around. Much calmer than I would expect of
her. Zara is a beautiful name. You must be pleased." said
the princess. "Well, I'm still getting used to her, but we do
have a lot of fun together" said Jester. "Good, soon enough
a time will come when your bond will be tested." She said
plainly. Jester suddenly had a hundred questions about
dragons, the sword and the crest, and…if he could kiss her
again. "I know I had interrupted some kind of 'ritual'
back in the forest that d…" The Grey Princess put a finger
to his lips. Her eyes met his. "What's done is done. It is
not possible by any means, to change the imprinting of a
dragon. Zara is a lifelong companion to you. Does that
idea sit well with you?" she questioned. To that, he had no
answer at all. "To tell you the truth, I had intended to end
her life just after her hatching. I just couldn't do it. If she

grows to be a large dragon, I have a big problem here. We definitely have a bond, and I'm not willing to end it now, or ever for that matter. She's stuck with me I'm afraid!" he laughed.

Chapter Eight

(The Dunvegan honour guard and a spectacle)

The morning, though bright, had a haze in the air likely from a distant fire. The honour guard horses stood at the ready. They had been bathed and brushed the night before. The light horse armour, more for show than protection, gleamed brilliantly in the dull sunlight. The leatherwork shone with fresh oil. Even the many buckles and fittings had been carefully polished to a near mirror finish! The men milled about in their honour guard chain-mail. Their helmets and light armour shone as brilliantly as the horses did. The standard bearers had the castle flags neatly pressed and mounted to the polished metal standards, ready for placement in the leather cups that were attached to the woven blankets of each of their horses. Jester entered the courtyard wearing his best tunic, leggings and shiny leather boots. He wore no armour on this occasion, but the new sword was on his belt, and of course Zara. The chief armourer had made a 'dragon' blanket for Zara out of copper. It was the greenish color of the natural metal and attached by a simple light chain around her lower neck. Jester had put it on her earlier in the morning. She had stared at it for quite awhile but seemed comfortable with it on her.

The sergeant, in his best commanding voice boomed, "Honour guard! Mount up!" Everyone mounted the horses almost in unison. "To Dunvegan manor!" The honour guard set of through the courtyard. The horses feet made the familiar loud clopping sounds on the cobblestones, changing abruptly as they crossed the heavy wooden bridge over the moat, and abruptly again as they met the dirt pathway. They turned northeast towards the forest and the highlands. The dull sunlight glinted off the various polished metals. Jester rode beside his friend. "Tell me sergeant, was that not a kind thing the armourer did in making Zara her own blanket?" The sergeant looked at Zara in her copper blanket. "It goes well with her color sir!" They both laughed. Periodically, Zara would turn and look at her blanket, then stretch out her wings and settle again, always nose first into the breeze.

The sergeant cleared his throat. "Sir, if I may ask, what will you do as little Zara begins to grow up? Surely she will be as large as our friend from earlier one day. You'll need a slightly larger bedchamber, and the castle doors will be immense. Upwards of two strong men to open, and close them sir." "Truthfully sergeant, I have not given any thought to that. I have no idea how long it takes a dragon to grow into adulthood. I have to admit though; Zara is quite a lot heavier than I first remembered." Both men laughed.

The ride through the forest and into the highlands was peaceful and uneventful. The men mostly kept to their thoughts. Not the usual banter on a ride like this. Most were likely tired from the night's festivities. They rode past the barren crossroads and turned left. Dunvegan manor was just a short ride away now. "Form up tightly now, look alive!" commanded the sergeant. The honour guard closed up the gaps between them and began a canter. The banners flew brightly as they proceeded towards the manor house.

Some of the other regions had their honour guards just outside the courtyard entrance. The men remained on the horses. Many different banners moved in the light breeze. Most were only six to the guard. Jester had twelve in his guard plus himself and the sergeant. They rode in unison into the field behind the other guards and formed up to the far right. Jester guessed over half the kingdom had sent an honour guard to the proceedings, with still more arriving. Soon the field was nearly full of honour guards representing the various regions of Tyde. The smell of fresh leather oil and the horses themselves filled the senses. He looked at the various banners hoping to see a crest similar to the one on his sword. In the courtyard proper, several horses bearing differing versions of the Dunvegan crest stood at rest. There riders inside the manor house. Shortly, a detail of Dunvegan's men brought wooden troughs out to each guard, followed by a cart of water for the horses and men. Lord Dunvegan's master-at-arms came on his horse to the front of the courtyard. "Stand down! Guards may speak easy! Lords, ladies and emissaries to the manor!" shouted the man. Jester dismounted. Zara moved to go with him. He hesitated briefly, and then extended his arm to Zara who ran to her place on his shoulder, wings outstretched. "Stay sharp sir." the sergeant advised. "Always" said Jester. He and Zara created a wide berth as they joined the others heading into the manor.

Lord Dunvegan and his daughters, Shandahr, and the Grey Princess, as well as his only son, Ronald (Somewhat touched it was said of him. He rarely spoke, and lived in his own world mostly), formed a line to receive each guest. The group before Jester each exchanged hugs with the family and proceeded further into the manor's greatroom. Jester and Zara approached Lord Dunvegan. He merely bowed to him, never taking his eyes off Zara.

Zara tightened her grip noticeably on Jester's shoulder.
Shandahr offered her hand which he kissed. Upon releasing
her hand, she gave his hand the merest of squeezes.
Unusual he thought. The Princess offered her hand and
he was about to kiss it when she pulled him close and
whispered in his ear to sit to the far right. She then kissed
his neck before raising a finger to Zara who happily rubbed
her muzzle against it. Jester looked into her eyes and gave a
quick nod, then headed into the nearly full greatroom.

When you have a dragon perched on your
shoulder it's easy to clear a path though a crowd. Jester
did as he was asked and sat at the far right of the room.
He laughed to himself at the empty chairs immediately
around him. Zara sat quietly and eyed the guests. Jester
had been on his horse for several hours and felt a little
uncomfortable. He stretched his arms upwards then
outwards and tilted his head back. He froze. High above
on the greatroom's ceiling was the most lifelike full relief
carving of an adult dragon he had ever seen. A female
he noted. The dragon was portrayed upside down as if it
were holding onto an unseen perch high above the floor. It
looked remarkably like the one he had attempted to rescue
the Princess from. The eyes seemed to stare back at him.
Very realistic workmanship. The carving's head tilted just
very slightly! Jester's heart raced in his chest. So this was
where it lived. Ahead on the end wall were two massive

panels built just below the cross bracing of the wall. Huge doors! Of course! How else would it gain access to this room with out destroying it? Uneasily he sat upright and looked over the gathering. No one had noticed the high ceiling's occupant. If they had, it would be as he had first thought, merely a relief carving. Nothing more! It was brilliant to hide it in plain sight. When seen from the room's entrance, it appears to be just part of a complex support structure.

The Dunvegan family walked down the center isle and proceeded to the front of the room. They faced everyone then sat. Shandahr guiding Ronald gently along and seating him before taking her place. Lord Dunvegan stood again. He cleared his throat. "Lords, ladies, emissaries! It is our heartfelt thanks for your attendance today in this sad and solemn proceeding…Many of you knew my wife in better days. She was the binding force of the household then. A good friend to all who knew her. A good wife, an even better mother. My daughters and…" He paused slightly. "Son are mourning her loss as we prepare her final journey. It is a task left to those behind, to uphold and carry out without fail. I would be a liar if I said her last years were pleasant, surrounded by family and close friends. I am relieved and grateful that she has taken the…" He paused again and glanced at his children. "The final step." He finished the statement but seemed

unable to continue. A murmur came from the crowd.
The Princess rose and steadied her father, his head bowed
as if defeated by the death of his wife. For the first time,
Jester felt empathy for Lord Dunvegan. If he were in his
boots, he'd feel at a loss for words too. In you're vows, it's
'until death do you part', its very different day from when
it finally happens for real. He wanted to stand up and
move about. The chair was uncomfortable and he wished
he could rejoin his men. Dunvegan and his Grey Princess
spoke quietly for a moment, and then Dunvegan sat down
finally. The Princess continued on his behalf. "Lords,
ladies and emissaries, please join us in the final step of
our mother's journey. Meet us at the grave marker shortly
to pay your last respects. In accordance with the ancient
laws we uphold, her body shall be sent to the ever after by
dragon fire. Those not wishing to witness this final loving
act, we thank you for your attendance today and wish
you a safe return home." said the Grey Princess almost
tonelessly. Jester looked upwards surreptitiously and noted
the ceiling art was fully awake now.

The crowd thinned as everyone proceeded out
the front doors into the bright sunlight. Jester and Zara
were the last to rise. The room was very quiet now. The
princess motioned for him to come to the front of the
room, rather than exit the way the others had. "My father
wishes a word with you, if you'd be so kind?" she asked.

"Certainly." Jester sat at the end of the front table. Zara stared at Dunvegan. "I wish to tell you a thing about your young dragon, if I may?" said Dunvegan. "Why yes sir, please do." said Jester, leaning forward. "Your crest on your sword bears two dragons. Both differing in their abilities, not only their parentage." Dunvegan looked upwards to the high ceiling. "If my daughter would be so kind?" The princess turned and looked upwards. She made a small motion of her left hand. The great dragon lowered her neck till the head touched the floor, then released its grip on the hidden perch and turned its body so it was upright. Using her neck and tail, she gently lowered her body to the floor. Zara was now staring at the adult dragon with great interest. She carefully left Jester's shoulder and made her way to the center of the table where she sat facing the other. Dunvegan cleared his throat. "Draw your sword and observe the crest again, tell me what you see?" asked Dunvegan. Jester thought some powerful magic was working on his eyes. He looked at the two dragons before him, then at the sword's crest. Somehow both dragons' necks were intertwined together. The chain-mail hand under both dragons as before, but now with the palm up, as if to hold them both! "It's changed sir. The dragons are joined at the neck and the hand holds both!" said Jester. He felt the shining metal crest with his fingers. How could this be? It was metal! Not easily altered. "This shows you the 'Hand of the

71

Dragon', an old crest long ago forgotten. It is told the kingdom's first dragon master had this crest for her own. Its bearer has the ability to control the balance of magic power, good and evil. One, or the other, unable to rise up and take control. All three of the crests elements must be present for this balance to happen. You have much still to learn from the little one. Use that time wisely my friend." Dunvegan slumped a little in his chair. It was as if the telling of this knowledge was a drain on him. "Father, it is time now." said the princess. She looked at Jester, "Gather your Zara and follow us please." She outstretched her arms and the two great doors slid open. Jester placed the sword back in its scabbard and Zara on his shoulder. Without another word they exited the manor and proceeded to where Lady Dunvegan laid wrapped in a white shroud. She was on a narrow flat stone in the open ground near the manor's outer guard wall. Most of the other attendees were now gathered there. As he suspected, there was no open grave in the rocky ground. The remaining Dunvegan family gathered at a 'safe' distance from the shrouded body. They held hands and began to speak words he could not hear. Presently a large shadow crossed the suns light. The onlookers gasped as the huge dragon shape crossed the sun a second time. With a great rush of air, the adult dragon landed heavily near the body in the white shroud. The grey princess approached the beast with out hesitation. It lowered its head and she ran her hand firmly along its jaw line. Just like Zara, only a lot bigger thought Jester. She spoke to the dragon, but he could not make out the words clearly. She took her place again by her family's side. The dragon craned its long neck upwards, over the shrouded body and opened her great jaws wide. A reddish yellow flame shot forth, lighting the shroud and contents on fire. Jester knew from firsthand experience with this dragon, it could get a lot hotter still! The shrouded body seemed to slowly vanish in the flames. Dragon fire is a persistent thing. At length, the guests took there leave and began their journeys home. Soon, only a handful remained, Jester among them. The Princess returned to the dragon. Again, lowering its head to hers. She stepped back and the dragon let out a great fire ball, far hotter than anything Jester had seen before. The remains were nothing more than a fine ash. The dragon's massive wings lifted it skyward, the ashes scattered from the down force of air from the powerful wing beats. Jester turned away from the blast of air. He noticed a tall oblong stone, tilted almost to the ground. There were many strange markings carved on it. It seemed out of place where it had sunk into the ground. Something seemed strangely familiar to him as he looked at it. He would ask Myra about it later. The dragon cleared the highest trees and disappeared from sight. There was no sign of there ever having been a shrouded body on the now cracked stone slab that held it. Zara had been frightened by the adult dragon's flame and had crawled into his tunic. She finally peeked out just as the Princess walked over to where Jester stood. She gently put her hands on his shoulders. "Shandahr is going to stay with my father and brother for a few days now. Would you stay awhile? I know it's unusual of me to ask that, but I'd like your company if you are comfortable with that." she asked. "My lady, I'd enjoy nothing more. Let me send the men home and I'll rejoin you at your manor." His eyes smiled back at hers. He walked back to the honour guard and told the sergeant to take the men back without him. "Sir, I remember you had a rather long walk home last time you visited." he said. "I'll just have to take my chances sergeant. She actually wants my company, by personal invite. I do, however, expect to be back later tonight." The sergeant shook his head slowly and smiled. "Very well sir, do try and stay out of trouble. Ah, the female kind sir." The sergeant winked at his friend. "Honour guard! For home!" shouted the sergeant. The guard rode smartly past him. They were the best turned out guard here he thought as they exited the courtyard onto the trail. He turned and got on his own horse. He reached into his tunic and placed Zara on the horse blanket in front of him. He carefully unclasped the small chain around her neck and removed the copper blanket from her. "Now you can be yourself young lady." At that, he laughed out loud. Zara turned into the breeze and they rode to the Grey Princess's home.

Chapter Nine

(The visit)

The Princess had just placed her horse in the paddock adjacent to the old house, its tack and blanket now removed. Jester and Zara dismounted outside the gate. Zara went off to do her business as Jester began to remove his horse's well polished ceremonial tack and blanket. He placed it all in the open box beside the gate. His horse pushed past him and into the field to enjoy the grass. Jester went over to the large stone slab the princess was sitting on. Zara was already there, sitting beside her. He was about to sit, when a large shadow crossed the sun again. The dragon turned sharply left as it cleared the manor's rooftop, its powerful rear legs far forward for landing. It raised its wings almost straight up to spoil the lift they provided and touched down in the courtyard before them. Jesters hand was already at his swords handle, a reflexive action only. He knew they were in no real danger. Even Zara seemed calmer and made no move to hide this time. He knew animals could sense impending danger well before humans could. The great wings folded along its sides and back as it exhaled loudly. The head swung around on its long neck till it was just a few feet away. Jester could feel its breath against his tunic. He remained completely still. The Princess rubbed its jaw with her hand. The head tilting slightly so she could push more firmly. Both its eyes closed momentarily, and then snapped open. It really was an unsettling gaze. After a moment the dragon settled onto its belly and placed its lower jaw flat out on the courtyard stone. The same as little Zara does when she is resting but not asleep. Jester looked at the Princess. "Well I see I'll be on my best behaviour here!" and laughed. She leaned over and kissed him. He couldn't help but kiss her back, but kept one eye on the resting beast at their feet. Zara was resting too. Stretched out in the same manner as the larger dragon. She stood and said, "I'm really hungry, would you join me at supper?" she asked, taking his hands in hers. Jester stood warily, she held his hand as they walked to the door and into her home. The dinning table was set for two he noticed. She touched a chair. "Please be seated. I'll bring the food." She disappeared into the pantry. A moment later she carried a large serving tray with all manner of foods on it and set it on the table. She crossed over to the window overlooking the courtyard and waved him over. Outside, Zara and the adult dragon remained resting in identical fashion. "She is in good company. They are learning from each other." she said. "Let us begin shall we?" They went back to the table and sat. He expected her to sit at the opposite end of the table but instead joined him by his side, even moving her chair slightly closer to him. The food was excellent. He was surprised how hungry he was. "Tell me, is all this, your own doing?" he gestured towards the table top. She regarded him with wide eyes. "Why yes sir, it is." she said formally, then winked back at him. "Just because I'm a princess, doesn't give me leave to ignore the culinary arts. Contrary to what you may have heard, I'm quite domestic really." She took another bite from her chicken leg, followed by a sip of red wine. He had never seen the Princess in such an everyday situation before. It's always been howling storms, thunder and lightning, and the massive dragon. He was enjoying the moment with her. It was as close to normal as it would ever be, he thought. She was very much her own person. She turned and looked at him. Such beauty he thought. He could happily get lost in those eyes. "Ask me." She said. "Ask me anything you want I'm feeling generous with answers tonight." she stated. "Princess, I..." she cut him off with a wave. "My name is Myra. You may call me by that if you wish." "Myra, how is it that you're still a single woman. I can't believe you have not married." asked Jester. She laughed, "My dear sir, you give me much credit and I thank you for that. I am 36 years of age. I have simply met none that suit my, taste, as it were. They are either too needy, or so wealthy, they feel their riches can buy my affections. Like you, I follow my heart and instincts in these matters. I have no time for mere triflers or wagon loads of gold. All, inconsequential. Time wasters, all of them." she said plainly. Jester was surprised by her age. Fully ten years older than he. It was of no concern though. Age is all relative, to a point. If she was 20 years his senior, he would still be attracted to her. He knew better than most men, true beauty was far deeper than mere skin tone and muscle. In reality, beauty was more an inner thing that required some effort and care, to discover, rather than a mere casual glance. "If I may ask, how did you end up with the dragon?" "It was not as spectacular as Zara's arrival in your life. She was found in an abandoned nest by my sister. She told me of its location and we went to see it. Curiosity mainly. I was twelve; she was nine at the time. There was a single egg, likely abandoned from the mother's death. Dragons do die, sadly. Much before their time, in some cases. We took the egg home and hid it in a stable. Not long after, a huge storm came through and lightening set the stable on fire. My sister and I tried to get to the egg but it was too hot to even get near it! A second and third bolt of lightening struck the same spot. My father and his men were finally able to put out the fire. Later that morning I found the baby in the ashes. She imprinted me before I knew it, and

here she is to this day." She gestured towards the window overlooking the courtyard. "My father is wise in the ways of magic and even dragons for that matter. There were many dragons in his time. He knew their ways more than anyone. He even wrote a book about them years ago. Truthfully I've only seen it once. It was in his reading room. A fire destroyed it years ago. A great loss to him I'm sure." She drank more of her wine. Jester was still taking this all in when she asked, "Tell me something of you? It's your turn brave knight!" she seemed to giggle at that. He cleared his throat and drank several large mouthfuls of the wine, emptying his glass. She refilled it as he began to speak. "I'm from a very wealthy family, wagon loads of gold I'm sure. During the Great War both my mother and father were captured and killed, the gold taken and the lands burned to ash. I was lucky; somehow my dear friend and I were able to get to a place of relative safety. I would have been near twelve at the time. A distant land owner figured out who I was and kept my friend and me as their own. It all worked out well in the end. I'll never forget their generosity. They too have since passed I'm afraid. The King knew who I was and bestowed my family crest and lands back to me after the war ended. I'm a knight pro…"
"Protectorate, I know this. Tell me about your ability with animals. Few people understand them like you! Even your annual party in their honour is amazing!" she exclaimed. He took another drink of wine and regarded her. "That

my dear Myra, I can't explain fully. Animals just know I'm not a threat to them. Since I can remember, all manner of cats, dogs, even a wolf pup, have followed me home, or befriended me in some way. They can sense I'm a kindred spirit some how." He laughed at this out loud. Myra got up and moved her chair so they were facing one another. "I'll return your question of me. You are still unmarried, is there a special someone?" Jester laughed a little too loudly. He regarded her for a moment. "Like you, I just haven't met anyone to share my life with. I figure she will just drop miraculously into my lap one day and that will be that. I have my own castle and troops, I'm well paid by the King, and I have my own horse. Now I even have a baby dragon, what's not to like?" he laughed. "In reality I have not made time for such things. My life is uncomplicated and I like who and what I am. When the right woman comes along, I'll know. Until then, I'll just keep an open mind." She leaned forward and took his head in both her hands. "You sir, are a gift. I sensed that the moment I met you." She looked straight into his eyes. "It's time you take 'The Next Step.'"

Myra and Jester entered the courtyard where both dragons rested. She placed Zara facing the adult dragon and had Jester kneel between them. The adult dragon stood, with its head lowered, as did Zara. "Place your hand on each dragons head, just in front of the eyes." She instructed from a distance. Jester did as he was asked. He could feel a strange sensation through his body. His head, in particular. It felt like cool water running from the large dragon, through him, into Zara. He could somehow see himself between the two dragons from high above, like a passing crow would see. Over the rooftop of, the old manor house, to the top of the stony hill, where he and Myra first kissed. There was the circular burn mark from the lightning strike that night. The view changed to the large clearing where he first laid eyes on Myra and the great dragon he now touched. The grass was just beginning to re-grow. A stag and his harem were grazing on the new grasses. Somehow he was able to now see below the grasses and soil. The trees were much smaller now. It was a dragon nest! Three eggs together, in a great earthen depression. The devoted female dragon sat nearby, guarding her treasures. A tall rectangular stone occupied the far end of the nest area, a strange but somehow familiar writing carved into its sides. The view changed again, this time from much higher up. Two armies marching towards the dragons nest. Jester felt weak suddenly. His arms dropped to his side. He collapsed between the dragons, hitting his head, soundly on the cobbled courtyard.

He awoke with a start! He was in a most comfortable bed. Pillows surrounded him, Zara asleep in a wad of bedding, her tail sticking out of one end. He was disoriented. This was not his bedchamber. It was tidy and smelled of roses! He sat up and realized he had a terrible headache. He slowly lay back down on the bed. The events of the evening before slowly came back to him one by one. The door opened and Myra entered the room with a tray of fruits and a drink for him. "Princess, I, I meant Myra, sorry, I'm really…" he trailed off. "Out of it, I'd say by the look of it. You took a blow to the head when you hit the ground last evening. I knew you'd survive but a close call all the same. I had to sew you up." "You didn't use your powers to heal this like my nose?" he inquired. "It was too much of a risk after your connection with the dragons. It could have altered what they have shown you thus far. I won't risk that with you. Besides, my sewing abilities are above average!" she laughed at that. "Your head must hurt my dear knight protectorate. Drink this. I mean all of it, then, eat some of this fruit. I'll be back to check on you shortly." At that, she quietly left the room. Carefully, Jester felt his head. A dressing was applied to the left side of his head. It hurt. He drank from the cup. A fowl tasting liquid, but he managed to finish it as ordered. He ate one of the pears on the tray and fell back asleep. His dreams were broken. Nothing began or ended. Like watching a play, with many interruptions. He could feel coolness on his face and head. He opened his eyes to see Myra with a wet rag sitting beside him, then blackness again. He dreamt he was just floating in cool water. He could hear a waterfall nearby. It was peaceful wherever he was. He tried to open his eyes but it required too much effort. He just laid back and let the water carry him.

His eyes opened again. It took a few moments to realize he was in the same bed again. His clothes hung carefully on a wooden bar across the room. Zara was still wrapped up in a sheet but on the opposite side from where he remembered. Her tail twitched with another Zara dream. He slowly turned his head away from Zara and saw Myra asleep beside him. She was on top of the covers wearing her familiar grey dress as always. He looked at the room's window. It was now dark outside. Only the sound of her steady breathing in the room. He turned slightly to face her and put an arm around her. He was asleep soon after. No dreams came to bother him that night.

The sun streamed though the window and across the bed. Jester awoke and squinted in the bright light. His head now felt much better. He stretched, expecting to feel the lump of Zara near his feet. He looked over the bed. No Zara. He felt well enough to sit up. His feet had barely touched the floor when he heard a woman's laughter somewhere distant in the manor. It was a real laugh, not a polite stifled one. He could hear Zara's trill afterwards.

Life was good again. He walked to the mirror and looked at himself. Both eyes were still slightly blackened, giving him a raccoon look. A small bandage was still wrapped around his head. All this from a simple fall? He had been through worse with never a lost moment. He'd lost track of how many days he'd been here. Surely the sergeant would have come by now. He gathered his clothes and dressed. Jester entered the hallway and headed for the stairs down to the greatroom below. A torn and shredded blanket hung from the railing. Definitely the work of Zara! Myra and Zara were in the manor's greatroom playing tug of war. From what he could see, Zara might just have the upper hand. Myra was leaning back at a step angle, both hands firmly around a large dusting cloth. Zara was on her belly, all four legs fully reversed, and her wings far forward for extra grip. Dragons by their nature have eight ways to hold onto things. They are blessed with two complete sets of shoulders. The four legs with powerful toes and sharp claws, the wings which can, and do, act as two extra legs when needed. The mid-wing joint also has a retractable, single claw for added gripping power. The jaws and neck form a very powerful means of grip. Dragons can lift or pull their own weight by using only the jaws and neck muscles. Lastly, their tail is very flexible and can hold the dragons full weight easily, or be used as an anchor point when possible. Only the female dragons can actually lock their tails to something, due to the reversed boney split at the end of the tail itself. Had there been a table leg handy, Zara could wrap her tail around it, and using the reversed split, lock herself to it, to prevent further slipping. Jester laughed at the two of them. Zara let go suddenly, causing Myra to land on the floor! Zara ran over to Jester and jumped into his arms, 'trilling' excitedly. "What a pair you two make!" laughed Jester. He set Zara back down onto the stone floor, and she ran to Myra making several smoke rings in the air as she did so. "I see your feeling human again. You took a very bad hit to the head. The single stone you landed on had a pronounced edge to it. Not all stones are created equally flat I'm afraid." said Myra. "Neither are the knight protectorates that strike them!" laughed Jester. "I should get back to my castle. My sergeant will be very upset with me." "He was here my protector, he checked in on you. I told him he could take you, but he didn't want to move you!" "That's ok my lady, I understand. How long have I been here?" he asked. "Fully three days now." she stated. "Three days? but the…" he trailed off. "Jester, don't force it, please. Your memory of the last few days will return soon enough, including what the dragons have taught you. There is still more to do though. Much more. You'll need some time to digest what you have learned so far. We will continue this, another time soon." she said quietly. "Why is it that I feel there is a 'plan' I'm unaware of. Something big is in the making, I feel it! The crest on my sword is unchanged from its new form, why is that?" he was puzzled and still feeling not himself yet. "I'll do my best to explain it thus far, please, sit with me in the courtyard." He followed her outside and they sat on the stone slab bench.

"At the time of the great war, our kingdom, Tyde, was almost overrun by another kingdom from across the great sea. A place called Ionica. A large and powerful army commanded by their ruler, Vectus, arrived at our shores and began to attack and enslave our people. Thousands upon thousands of our citizens were either taken away or killed, like your parents. They destroyed everything in their path, laying waste to everything. It took an effort of unimaginable force, with magic and knowledge from certain key people, known as the chosen, for their abilities to carry and use the magic to finally repel Vectus back to the sea and force his return to Ionica. The dragon's played a key role in this. It took nearly twelve months to bring that about. Since then, some of the chosen vowed to keep and maintain this power if ever another attempt was to be made to take our kingdom from us. My father is one of them. Not many from those days still live, so the base of power has begun to thin out. This 'balance' has been very difficult to maintain over the years and is now on the verge of becoming lost to us if we cannot maintain our strength. You've seen yourself what its doing to my

father! He can no longer carry his share of the weight
left to him as more, just like him, pass away. He tried to
transfer some of his power to our mother. She was not
able to absorb what he gave her. She was left an empty
shell after the transfer. As you know, she never recovered
from it. We have since learned, by accident, this transfer
is unsafe to most. The dragons however can and do take
the transfer well, but it's only storage of sorts. Someone
needs to be able to take that power and put it to use when
and if the time ever comes again. Several have tried. My
dear brother Ronald tried. Although not affected like
my mother, he too has suffered from its weight. His head
could not deal with it well, and you know the rest." She
paused, and looked at him. "So you think I may be able
to 'carry' some of this power?" asked Jester. Myra looked
him directly in the eyes. "Not just some of it, all of it."
she said simply. Jester looked away from her. "You realize
that you're becoming the next dragon master. Only a rare
few can do this. At the time of the Great War, no one
had the inner ability to do this by themselves." Things
were becoming even more confusing, rather than clearer.
"It is possible then I'll become like Ronald, or worse,
your departed mother?" he looked into her dark eyes. "I
can tell you only that is a possibility. I can also tell you
that your way you have with the animals is something
different from Ronald or my mother. They did not have
the 'connection' you have with them. Zara, for example,

is more a part of you than you know at this time. Even
Tantrus, my own dragon, could have killed you instantly
the day we met abruptly in the fire. She resisted doing
that, knowing what she carries with her. She sensed your
ability immediately. She just 'knew'!" Jester was just able
to keep up with all of this. His mind working to make
sense of what Myra was telling him. "When I healed your
broken nose that day, I too, knew what you were capable
of. I felt it in you clearly, aside from you wanting to kiss
me then." she smiled at him. "I still do." he said and they
kissed. "The old storyteller woman said it was a matter
of the heart. Even the dragons had to agree to it before it
was done." Suddenly Jester stood. "Wait, it's a map. The
dragons have given me a map! I know what it is now!" said
Jester excitedly. "Then it has begun. I think we need to
do this in small steps, not all at once!" said Myra. "You're
doing well so far, I don't want to damage you in anyway.
I could not bear that. Your passing out during the map
transfer was likely a good thing. A self preservation of
sorts." She stood finally and they moved to the hearth
in the manor's greatroom. "Tell me, is Zara from an egg
by Tantrus? Are they the same breed?" asked Jester. "It's
a long story. You came in near the end of it." she said.
She sat down in a large stuffed chair and motioned for
him to sit in the adjacent one. He sat and ran his hand
over the top of his head, pulling his hair away from his
forehead. "In a word, no. Zara is not of Tantrus, they are

very different breeds. Zara is unusual in that she is a small dragon. Normally she would be much larger since her hatching. My father can tell you more about her, I'm sure. I can tell you this. The very earliest dragons were very small in stature, like Zara. They were pure creatures of the wind and sky. It is told that they are the best natural fliers. Their kind held the balance of powers for centuries. They were the only dragons to ever have wilful contact with humans. They were able to teach the humans about the importance of maintaining the balance of good and evil powers. Please, ask my father, he knows so much more than I on these matters. Zara's egg was found, again, by my sister. It was abandoned in its nest many years ago. By chance, she came across it while walking on the great rocky hill. It looked like it could be just another rock, but she has an eye for these things apparently. She brought it home and gave it to me. I decided we could hatch the egg with the help of dragon fire. The little one was to imprint with her, at least that was the idea. Then you came in and changed everything. I, for one, didn't think Shandahr was capable of handling the power any more than my mother, or Ronald could. It somehow worked in everyone's favour. It was a most fateful of days. You see, it is the dragons who recognise and choose who will become the dragon master. It is a shared power between the dragon master and all dragons." She regarded Jester sitting in the chair. A strong impulsive man, driven by his heart. She hoped the power would leave him unchanged. For all her powers of magic, both light and darker, even she couldn't know the outcome of that. Her strong attraction to him muddied the view even more. Now she found that her choice was also one of the heart. He would become a dragon master. The first in over a hundred years. It was a new feeling for her, once long ago forgotten.

Chapter Ten

(Small troubles lead to bigger ones)

Jester turned his horse at the now familiar barren crossroads and headed towards the castle. Zara seemed to doze on her perch. They had hugged their temporary goodbyes. He sensed Myra was somewhat saddened by his departure. Lost in thought, the pair continued in silence, only the steady sound of the horse's foot steps on the sandy trail.

The horse suddenly stopped dead in its tracks. Jester nearly fell off the frightened animal. Zara fluttered her wings and backed up into Jester's waist. The horse snorted and tossed its head and turned. Jester pulled on the reins hard to prevent it from bolting. They were about mid forest at this point. The shade from the canopy high above was almost complete. Clearly something or someone was nearby. The horse was alert and nervous. Jester looked at its ears pointed straight ahead. He dismounted and

placed Zara on his shoulder. Quietly he walked the still
frightened horse back from where they had come and tied
it off to a stout tree well clear of the path. He carefully
unsheathed his sword and made his way back parallel to
the pathway. He made almost no sound as he continued
slowly through the trees. He finally caught sight of some
movement just ahead of him. He ducked down and
moved along a wide circular clearing. He managed to
crawl to the edge of the clearing and saw a small troop of
eight men in full battle armour. They had no horses and
little equipment with them. He'd never seen such dull
black armour before. Even their faces were painted dark,
like their armour. They spoke in a language he did not
know. There was no banner or crests to be seen at all. They
had no guard posted for lookout either. The focus was
on the several rabbits cooking over a small fire they had
made. Rather than broadswords, they were armed with
crossbows. Much smaller than the longbows, they were
more for mid-range fighting. This was an advance scouting
party no doubt. As to what they might be scouting, and
more importantly, for who, was a mystery. Jester quietly
circled the makeshift camp till he was behind the men
now enjoying their rabbit meal. A helmet had been left
carelessly close to the brush and he was able to just reach
it without being heard. He made his way back to the horse
and examined the helmet. It was indeed completely black.
It had no markings of any kind and was very strong.

He had a bad feeling about this. Before he untied his horse and walked it to the path, he tied the helmet to the padded horse blanket. The only easy way to the castle was straight down this path. It would take another full day to circle this part of the forest and get back. Those men were clearly alone and eating now. He grabbed Zara and mounted his horse. He put his heels into its flanks and the startled horse took off at full gallop. He would be past them before they could react and onwards to the castle! As he neared the spot adjacent to the camp his horse struck a trip rope carefully strung across the path and anchored to the trees on either side. The horse went down on its left side and slid fully twenty feet on the smooth path. Jester was able to roll off the animal to one side. Zara hurtled on straight ahead; her wings outstretched giving her a short glide into the heavy bushes up ahead. Jester was on his knees and about to get up when he was surrounded by the black armoured men. All eight crossbows aimed at his head. He held up his hands and slowly stood up. His horse got to its feet and bolted down the path towards home. Rider less yet again!

The man whose helmet was still tied to his horse gestured towards the trees. Jester began to walk in that direction, hands still held high. The bareheaded one reached forward and removed his sword. They came into the clearing with one rabbit dropped into the fire now and charred beyond any possibility of eating. They exchanged words with one another in their strange language. One man kicked the fire over and began stamping out the burning twigs. Another two began collecting their belongings. The bareheaded man examined Jester's sword. He held it high with some effort. The sword shook slightly. He dropped his crossbow and grasped the sword with both hands. It was with much effort he was able to hold it upwards. The strain beginning to show on his face and neck. He grimaced and put all he had into it to maintain his position with the sword. He shook from the sheer strength it took. His knees began to give from the force the sword applied to him. Suddenly the blade stuck him on top of his head. He was lucky it was the side of the blade, not an edge. It would have easily split him in half. He dropped to the ground stunned by the immense force of the blow. The five men watching took a step back, away from the sword. The man on the ground rolled over onto his knees and got up, holding his head with both hands now. He yelled at the five in their rapid sounding tongue and they raised the crossbows to Jesters head again. The bareheaded man strode to Jester and lifted him just off the ground by his tunic. In that moment, Zara dropped from the tree high above and streaked past them, a bright flash followed a moment later. The five crossbow armed men were on fire! Dropping their weapons and madly rolling and waving at the flames. The bareheaded man was startled and eased his powerful grip on Jester. He slammed his head into the big mans face with all his might, shattering his nose and followed up with a well placed knee to his inseam. He dropped like a soft child's doll in a heap at Jester's feet. Jester held his right arm out towards his sword shining in the grass. It flew to his hand in an instant. Zara narrowly managed a steep turn through the heavy tree trunks and landed on one of the remaining two men's helmet. His helper saw the dragon perched on his comrade's head and using sign language, put a finger to his lips. The other man froze, both eyes looking straight up. His helper swung at the dragon with his crossbow and squarely hit the other on the side of his head, knocking him unconscious. Zara simply jumped onto the others helmet. As he was reaching up to grab at Zara, a brilliant, silver blade just touched his throat. He dropped his crossbow to the ground, and raised his hands high. With Zara standing guard, Jester gathered the trip rope from the path and had all eight men tied in such a manner with various slip knots that if one struggled, the others knots would tighten further. Extremely uncomfortable, very effective. He had all their black armour in a pile by the pathway. Zara burned all but one of the crossbows. They didn't have long to wait till the sound of a full troop of his men at speed could be heard down the path. Jester unsheathed his sword again and pointed it at the bigger man. "You sir, have some explaining to do to. I hereby arrest all of you in the name of the King of Tyde. You are now my prisoners." he said as officiously as he could. The sergeant and his men rode to a halt in the path and dismounted. "Nice of you to attend, sergeant. Have them interrogated at the castle when you arrive. They all need medical attention, except one." "Sir, where is your help, the other men involved in this capture?" asked the sergeant. "Oh, yes, quite right sergeant, Zara? Come take a bow for the men!" shouted Jester. One of the black helmets detached itself from the pile of armour and zigzagged up to the sergeants boots and bumped to a stop. A muffled 'trilling' sound echoed from within. The sergeant looked wide eyed at Jester. "Who knew?" shrugged Jester.

It was good to be back in the castle, thought Jester. He made a beeline to the sausage and bun vendor in the courtyard. He and Zara took eight of them back to the greatroom and ate their fill. Jester wanted to sleep awhile before chatting with the sergeant in regard to the scouting patrol he encountered in the forest. It had been years since any military patrols, other than his own were on his lands. Something was up, and he wanted answers. There were experts who could likely speak the strange language of those men. It would not go well for them if they refused to talk. He would order regular patrols of his lands beginning tomorrow. He would also send

news of this encounter to all the knight protectorates
in the kingdom. He would ride to see the King the day
after tomorrow. His lands did border the great sea to the
west, and so did several others. A search for any ships or
longboats was in order. Every inch of coastline was to be
searched. He would also offer a gold reward for any useful
information in this matter. Satisfied with his plans so far,
he slept finally. He dreamt of Zara. Now fully three stone
in weight of fearless fire breathing fury! He smiled in his
sleep.

Zara had really saved the day. She had acted
without fear and instinctively knew she had to help him.
Lighting up the five men with crossbows was brilliant.
Just enough fire to occupy them fully. Any burns they
may have suffered were from their armour getting heated.
Dragon fire is a persistent thing! Her flying abilities were
improving too. It won't be long till she will be able to fly at
will, rather than a controlled glide from a tall place.

Jester was woken by the familiar pounding on
the bedchamber door. "Sir, I have some information on
the men captured in the forest." stated the sergeant. Jester
opened the door and went to the greatroom's table. "Have
a seat, what news?" he asked. The sergeant sat at one end
and regarded his friend for a moment. He leaned forward,

looking slightly uncomfortable. "Sir, I think there is something terrible coming our way. I had several of our men who understand many languages pose as others who were arrested for various crimes. We locked them up in a nearby cell. They did the usual claims of innocents to the guards and we left them. The men from the forest eventually began to talk amongst themselves. One of our men recognised the language as an old and rarely spoken tongue. He believes these men are from Ionica! They have only been here for a few days. As you suspected, I believe they are part of an advance scout of the kingdom. If this is true, their may be others." The sergeant looked uncomfortable with this information. Jester leaned forward and lowered his voice. "Sergeant, if what you say is even half correct, we are looking at the possibility of another invasion attempt. Sometime soon, I would think. A month, maybe two at best." "What will we do with the prisoner's sir?" he asked, raising his eyebrows. "Keep them for now sergeant. I'd like them separated and held so they can't talk to each other, and maintain a guard at all times. A second guard will bring the food and water; no one is to see them. I'd like a chat with the man who knows of their language." "He is waiting outside sir; I knew you would ask me that." The sergeant rose and crossed to the greatroom doors. He returned with a member of the troop, still dressed as a non-military man. "Please have a seat with us." He pointed to a chair opposite him and his sergeant. "What do you make of these prisoners? Speak freely." said Jester. "Sir, they speak an old toung not heard in these parts for many years. Not since the Great War I believe. I swear to you it's spoken by the soldiers from Ionica! I know this only by my father who knew many tongues himself. He fought in the Great War. He and a few others advised the Kings men during that time. He taught me the words to it. My father told me a time might come when this ability would be useful." "Your father was a wise man. What rank are you?" asked Jester. "I'm a standard bearer sir. I was in the honour guard for Lord Dunvegan. I…I even saw the great dragon sir! At the end, before we left." he said. Jester looked at his sergeant. "Promote this man to scout status, and swear him in." Jester then looked at the surprised man. "Not a word to anyone, including your friends in the troop, or family. For now, this situation is to be kept quiet till we can make further plans. Are you good with that?" The new scout stood. "Thank you sir, I'll do my very best!" The sergeant then stood. "Right then, we have some business to take care of. Follow me." He winked at Jester as he and the new scout left the table. Jester remained seated. This was not sitting well with him at all. He would notify the King in person. A movement at the bedchamber door caught his attention. The door opened just slightly. Zara wedged her nose into the opening and pushed through into the greatroom. She saw Jester seated at the table and made a smoke ring. It was larger than the ones she was previously able to make. Suddenly the ring ignited! A bright blue ring of fire danced before her, and then disappeared! She 'trilled' in excitement as Jester over tilted his chair and fell backwards onto the floor with a crash. He quickly picked himself up and righted the chair. "Well well, someone's been practicing new things I see!" Zara then lowered her head till it touched the floor. Her wings spread wide, and she jumped into the air. Flapping wildly, she made it to the table and landed. With her wings still unfolded, she walked over to a surprised Jester and 'trilled' again, tilting her head slightly. "You never fail to amaze me Zara. Did Tantrus show you that?" he said to her in a serious voice. Zara 'trilled' again and walked a slow circle to show herself off. Jester suddenly noticed what Zara was trying to show him. Behind her head, two boney points had formed. She was beginning to grow her dragon horns. The horns varied from dragon to dragon, even amongst the same breed, the horns were unique to the dragon. His Zara was becoming more capable and adult like. He picked her up and sat with her in his lap. Still thinking of the possibility of another invasion force preparing to leave Ionica. His thoughts were interrupted with two knocks at the greatroom door. The sergeant entered and walked over to Jester and Zara. "Are we to notify the King Sir? I can have a troop ready at anytime you wish." he said. "Have a seat sergeant. Yes we will ride to the Kings city tonight.

I want this matter kept quiet for another day or so. We will return shortly after our visit with the King. Any word from our patrols?" The sergeant cleared his throat. "Nothing to report at all sir. Most of the messengers have returned from the protectorates lands as well. Only the farthest reaching ones still due back Sir. I think we'll know soon enough if there are others hiding in our lands. There are already some rumours with the men sir. They know something is up." "It's alright sergeant. It's been a very quiet time for them these past years. They will be quick to jump on anything that remotely sounds like action for them. Have a dozen men at the ready just before sundown. Light armour, full weapons. I don't want any surprises on the ride out or back." The sergeant nodded and left without a further word. Jester held Zara up to him. "You ready for a fast night ride?" Zara 'trilled' and wiggled and squirmed. He set her down on the floor and she ran to the bedchamber. A moment later, returning with her copper armour in her mouth. Jester laughed, "I take that as a yes!" He picked Zara up and placed her on the table, then sat down in front of her. She dropped the copper blanket to the table and pushed it towards him with her nose, then turned around and sat. Jester was dumbfounded! She was waiting for him to place it on her back and fasten it. Zara never ceased to amaze him. In a moment she was ready. She climbed to his shoulder and they left for the courtyard below.

Chapter Eleven

(Darkening skies)

The men were already mounted and ready. A groom held Jester's lightly armoured horse at the ready. The sergeant had the blankets with the new crest on each rider's horse. Only a single banner flew on this ride. It was to be a fast trip without the usual fanfare. Jester mounted his horse, Zara on her perch in front. The sergeant held his gloved hand high briefly, and then lowered it in an arcing movement. The troop rode out the gates and turned away from the forest path towards the sea. The pace was a steady canter.

Zara loved being out at night. A dragon's vision is equally suited for darkness. They have an ability to use a light intensifier in their eyes that allows them to see very well in darkness. It was a half moon this night and the path was firm and wider than the forest paths. The troop made good time to the King's border. Twin towers of stone marked the boundary clearly. Jester could almost smell the ocean now. The path began to descend to the coast. It became more winding a route till finally they arrived onto a wide flat shoreline. Zara could see small crabs scuttle away from the troop as it rode onwards to the King's city. The breeze was straight off the water now and the smells were new to her. It was low tide now and the waves against the shore were further out. Jester loved the smell of the ocean. He would like to bring the Grey Princess here one day. He hoped for word on when the next learning session would happen with her. The sergeant suddenly raised his fist into the air. The troop stopped in their tracks. The sergeant dismounted and waved for Jester to follow him with several others. They walked to the waters edge. In the darkness Jester could just make out several longboats sunken in the shallow waters. Anything that would float was tied down carefully. It looked like maybe thirty some odd men could have landed on this shore, sank the longboats for a way to hide them in the open, and gone out on foot. The sergeant looked at Jester. "Sir, those men in our dungeons are not working alone." He waved the troop to come over on their horses. They quietly pulled the longboats out of the water onto the beach. The sergeant was right. Each boat was equipped with a plug to allow it to be refloated quickly and rowed out to sea again. They had five boats pulled up on the shore now. "Sir, we can't just leave the boats here." said the sergeant. "Zara could make short work of them, but too much attention with the fires!" "Actually sergeant, that is not entirely true. Let me show you something." said Jester. With that, he pulled all the plugs from the boats, and the oars and placed them in a pile near the waters edge. He then placed Zara near the pile and made a circle motion to her, then pointed at the pile. Zara produced a large smoke ring close to the pile of wooden objects. Every one watched closely. The ring of smoke almost surrounded the pile of oars and wooden plugs. Suddenly it ignited with a dull 'woof' sound. The resulting flash was bright but went out as fast as it had appeared. The pile was reduced to ashes in seconds. No fires, no sound. The sergeant looked at the barely smoking pile of ash, then to Zara. His eyes were wide in amazement. He then looked at Jester and turned his palms upwards. Jester nodded towards the Kings city. The troop remounted and continued their journey in silence. The sunrise was still a ways from breaking when they entered the Kings city.

Guards were posted everywhere. There was a real sense of purpose to all the activity in the main courtyard and the plaza in front of the Kings keep. The keep was designed to repel any and all attackers. It was the oldest building in the kingdom. It had been repaired and renovated throughout the years. Its walls were easily 10 feet thick, built of stone that interlocked front to back.

The most powerful of blows to the wall would fail to cause a breach in its sound design. The troop dismounted in the plaza, where several of the Kings grooms, led the horses away to the stable and water. Zara hissed at one groom about to take Jester's horse. He fainted on the spot. Collapsing in a heap on the century's worn cobble stones. Jester and the sergeant picked the young man up and draped him over Jester's horse. Zara ran to her place on his shoulder, while another 'braver' groom led his horse away. They met up with the King's sergeant-at-arms and they proceeded into the keep to the main hall.

The King, along with his many bearded advisors and a few emissaries, sat at a huge rectangular table, all of nearly forty feet long. Its surface covered in maps of the kingdom. The sergeant-at-arms cleared his throat. "Your grace, your western- region, knight protectorate, his sergeant, and...and dragon!" At that, all thirty some- odd men stopped and stared at Zara. She happily opened her wings to their fullest extent, blocking Jester's view, and blew a smoke ring towards the stunned gathering. Jester stepped forward and pulling Zara's left wing away from his face, bowed deeply, as did his sergeant. "Jester! You're the man of the hour. What news do you bring us?" said the King, in a deep, rough voice. Everyone at the planning table sat quietly and regarded Zara. Still in disbelief. "My King, we just found longboats very near the city. Hidden in the low tidal waters, not a mile from here. Our 'visitors' will not be returning the way they have arrived on our shores, I assure you. I firmly believe we are in a pre-invasion of the kingdom sir. I personally have taken eight men into custody on my lands. They speak a language from across the sea. We have reason to believe they are advance scouts from, well, Ionica sir." The main hall was completely silent. Everyone just looked at each other, then back to Jester and the sergeant. At length, the King spoke. "We have had no reports of anyone or anything out of the ordinary. Nor any fighting or skirmishes that we are aware of. You are to return to your lands and ready yourselves for whatever may come. Any word will come by my messengers as needed. Oh, and Lord Dunvegan has an urgent request that you attend his residence as soon as possible. Above all, keep vigilant. These may be dangerous times ahead for all of us. I bid you a safe and speedy return." The meeting table returned to its many conversations. The sergeant-at-arms led them back to the plaza where their horses and the troop waited.

They rode briskly out of the city gates and headed back the way they had come. It was early morning now and the wide tidal flats were again under water. Had they left any later that morning they never would have found the longboats in the shallow waters. They rode hard down the path to make as good a speed as possible without exhausting the horses. It was near mid afternoon that they reached the castle gates. The sergeant began organizing guards and archers to their stations. A full alert was in place. The watchtowers were manned continuously now. All the farms in the land were set up with large brush piles for use as signal fires should the need arise. Jester changed horses and left again for Dunvegan manor. He and Zara would arrive before nightfall.

Lord Dunvegan paced back and forth in his library. A great deal of large, partially un-rolled scrolls littered his writing desk. Most were line drawings of dragons. Myra sat in a large wooden chair in front of a huge book case, absorbed in her thoughts, when the sound of hooves clattering onto the courtyard startled them both. Myra got up and ran to the window. Jester was dismounting from his horse and Zara, wings flapping with excitement, perched on his right shoulder. The door opened as he approached it, and Myra ran to him and they kissed. "Thank you for coming so quickly!" she said breathlessly. "My father has much to tell you. So do I" Jester took her arm and they entered the manor. Zara wasted no time in getting her finger rub from Myra, then, jumped onto her shoulder. They walked straight to the library where Lord Dunvegan was arranging some of the scrolled parchments with the drawings. "Jester! Welcome! You must be thirsty after such a day on horseback. Myra produced a goblet of ale which he drank in one continuous motion. "Another, if I may?" he asked, returning the empty goblet to Myra. Lord Dunvegan had never called him Jester before now. Interesting, he thought. Dunvegan was always down to business, few, if any pleasantries were exchanged. He did like the friendlier version much better. "Thank you my Lord. You're quite right, it has been a long and swift day for me. I've been to see the King, and things are looking much darker. Advance scouts from what I believe to be Ionica have been found on our lands." Lord Dunvegan regarded Jester. Myra handed him a full goblet again. "I have been aware of this for a time now. I could not voice my concerns to anyone lest they think I'm just an old fool. Dabbling in various magic and childish potions. As you can see, that is not the case at all. I also have come to appreciate your ways my friend. Myra has been good enough to tell me of your progress in the very old and dangerous power we have carried all these years. I don't mind telling you, I'm relieved to hear how well you are taking it all in. I would like to transfer more to you this very night, if you are in agreeance? I'm afraid there may not be much time afforded to us now" he stated. Jester looked to Myra, she nodded at him. "Then I see no reason to delay matters. Let's get on with it, shall we?" said Jester.

They made their way to the main hall. Tantrus was resting on the floor, her gaze following every move. She lifted her head up from the floor when Zara fluttered down from Myra's shoulder. Both dragons touched their noses to each other and Zara circled once, and then settled a few feet from Tantrus. Myra squeezed jester's hand. "If this becomes too much for you just release your hand from either dragon. There are no sharp stones here. As before, the dragons will connect with you and the transfer will continue. Don't try to make sense of anything while this takes place, just let it happen." Myra motioned for him to kneel. He placed one hand on Zara's head and the other on Tantrus. Almost immediately, Jester could feel the connection begin. The same coolness flowing through his hand that touched Tantrus, then passing through him into Zara. His feel of the present slipped away quickly and was replaced with more visions. A remote and rocky coastline appeared, with many large ships. A messenger arriving at his castle, bloody and injured, with a nearly ruined message from the king. Fire and smoke blotted out the sun. A very tall man standing on the beach, wearing a long, heavily armoured cloak with raven feathers on the shoulder, and black helmet. Behind him a dragon with dull black scales, wings raised to take flight. High vantage point with many armies fighting far below. Now several other dragons in the sky. Circling, their fire hitting one army. Picture after picture flooded his thoughts. It was

breathtaking and terrifying all at once! He began to feel
faint again. He dropped his hands from the dragon's
heads. Slowly the room came into focus again. He was
still kneeling! He hadn't passed out. He could see Myra
and Lord Dunvegan watching him. His head cleared
after a moment and he felt himself again. He stood.
Myra took him by his hand and sat him in a chair. The
dragons continued to remain where they were. He felt
as if he could sleep soundly now. Perhaps digest the new
information he 'learned'. It was pitch black out side. The
transfer must have taken some time, but did not feel that
way to him. "You did well, I half expected you to collapse
again. Your strength is more than we imagined! Well done
my knight!" said Myra. Jester felt a little weakened but,
otherwise was fine. He smiled at that! He looked at Zara,
nose to nose with Tantrus. The horns on her head had
grown proportionally to those of the much larger dragon.

Chapter Twelve

(Discovery)

Jester needed to rest for awhile. His head was full of new ideas and many images. He needed some time to digest them. Lord Dunvegan put a hand on his shoulder. "You have done exceedingly well young man! The transfer went quite nicely I think. You are very close to having it all! Well done. When you have had some time with these things, we do need to talk again." He smiled, pleased with the evenings outcome. Myra took his arm and led him back to the library. "I want you to stay till tomorrow. You need to rest, and you may have some questions that either I or my father can answer for you. Clarification is important." she said. Jester looked at her and smiled. "Careful my Princess, I'm a knight protectorate, and not easily swayed!" he laughed. Zara 'trilled' her part. They both laughed at that. Without a further word, Jester, with Zara on his shoulder, and Myra quietly got on their horses and rode to Myra's place for the remainder of the evening. They didn't talk at all during the ride. Jester felt drained of all energy now, and was trying to come to terms with how he felt, now that he had a great deal of 'new' insights into the power he was now carrying. The new visions raced in his mind, yet somehow felt like he had always had them.

They arrived in the tidy courtyard, just outside of the manor house and dismounted. The two horses were turned out into the adjoining paddock and began to graze on the short grasses that grew there. A sound of rushing air caught his attention. Although it was dark, he knew that Tantrus was making her wide turn over the manor's roof top, prior to landing. Moments later a great rush of air buffeted them as the huge dragon settled to the ground, its great wings nearly vertical. Tantrus exhaled loudly as she folded her wings against her sides and settled on the cobblestones. Jester was still in awe in her presence. He couldn't imagine Zara at that size. Without thinking, Jester walked up to the great dragon and rubbed his hand along her jaw line, just like Myra did. She tilted her head slightly towards Jester and pushed gently back. His touch was tolerated in a friendly way. He couldn't imagine in his wildest dreams of ever being able to do this to a dragon. It was simply unthinkable. His natural fear seemed to have left him now. It had been replaced by a deep respect for the dragon's intelligence and powers still to be learned.

Myra smiled, "I'm impressed, the last knight to get that close to her was cooked and eaten!" "She knows I'll taste awful and spit me out!" laughed Jester. Myra placed a hand on Tantrus's head and closed her eyes. After a moment she turned to him and looked into his eyes. Jester was dumbfounded. "I, I know what you just did I think. You let her know that she has done well. Tantrus has accepted me. Not in words like we speak to each other. She knew. A feeling more like an understanding. Do I make any sense?" Myra smiled back and nodded. "A dragon can feel what you wish to communicate. They understand much. Just a touch to their head and they feel what you feel, Zara can communicate with you also, although her thoughts and understanding are more advanced than you may think, it will be different from Tantrus. You have the knowledge, now you must learn how it all works through you. She turned to go back to the manor. Zara ran to the door and 'trilled'.

They entered the greatroom and sat across from each other in the large stuffed chairs near the hearth. Zara, as usual, went off to explore things. Jester removed his sword and scabbard to sit down and felt a sudden warmth at his side. It seemed to emanate from his sword. He slowly withdrew his sword and noticed the handle was warm to the touch, but the crest had changed to the entwined dragons and the gloved hand to the palm

up position again. This meant something, he knew it.
Myra spoke, "It's changed again. Do you know why?"
Jester continued to examine the crest. "I think I do now,
it's because of our situation at this point. My new found
knowledge, being able to touch Tantrus without fear, and,
and you Myra." Jester felt something was missing from
his explanation of the crest's change. "That's a good start
my brave knight, but what about, me? Surely not because
I sit here before you in the same room!" she laughed and
winked at him. She crossed her arms and maintained
direct eye contact with him. She was waiting. Without
warning, a vision of himself, engulfed in dragon fire
came to him. He stood in the inferno calmly, unharmed
by the flames. He raised an arm high over his head and
then brought it down quickly. The dragon fire stopped
suddenly. "Do you find it quite warm in here?" he asked,
trying to buy more time before he answered. Zara jumped
into his lap and flapped her wings at him, then fell over
backwards. She managed to roll over again and ran off to
the end of the greatroom, disappearing into the darkness.
Myra tried not to notice Zara's playfulness. "So, was that
everything you could think of then? Our 'situation' and
me?" she drummed her fingers on her crossed arms and
raised an eyebrow just slightly. He was about to speak
again when Zara hurtled past them. Wings up, and
flapping, goose like and disappeared into the darkness
once again. They both could hear her little claws on the

stone floor as she chased imaginary creatures around
the room. Jester cleared his throat, "I, meant to say that
the situation is not so much a situation but a, a feeling
that we, err, I felt, well, still do of course. I, I'm sure that
things are well, positive…" He was struggling with his
feelings towards Myra. He could command a troop of
men in any situation. Make life or death decisions without
pause. But this was different. This was a feeling he had
never really dealt with before. Zara flew past his head.
Close enough to blow his hair across his face, obscuring
his sight. She banked hard to the right, narrowly missing
the stair railings, then shot upwards and crashed into
the great iron candle holder above Jester and Myra,
causing it to sway wildly. She slipped through the ornate
metalwork and clung bat-like, upside down, struggling
to maintain her grip on the ornate ball at the bottom of
the holder. Jester was looking straight up at Zara amongst
the candles. Myra, eyes rolling, got up and sat on Jester's
lap facing him. She gently took his head in her hands.
"Just say it!" Jester blinked twice, then held her gaze and
said "I love you." Myra regarded him a moment and said
simply, "I know." At that moment Zara lost her grip on
the iron candle holder and dropped heavily beside them.
She bounced off the padded arm of the chair and knocked
the tools for the hearth over in a loud crash. With wings
outstretched, she hissed loudly at the still rolling poker.
It continued its slow roll towards her. She jumped up and

wedged herself between them and let out a muffled 'trill'. They both laughed. Jester finally said, "Please tell me Tantrus doesn't still play games like this!" "Oh she does though. But only outdoors." Jester's eyes widened. "She will fly low over the trees and grab a part of the tree top and carry it high up with her, then drop it. She will then chase it as it falls downwards and set it on fire at the last moment. Some times she will carry several at once and chase them all down before they get turned into ashes. It's a way of not only playing but more to keep their flying skills sharp. Few humans ever get to see such things."

Myra stood and crossed over to a large wooden box along the wall. She opened its lid and reached inside. "My father sent these. He wanted you to see them." She returned with a bundle of scrolled papers. "Come to the table, we can unroll them there." Jester picked up Zara and followed her to the dinning table where they unrolled the scrolls. Zara was placed on the end of the table. Beautifully drawn pictures of dragons appeared. Jester was amazed at the many different kinds of dragons that were represented. He carefully looked at each drawing in turn. He recognized Tantrus several pictures later. He continued through them but no 'Zara' dragon was represented. There was a black dragon with two heads and necks. He paused at this drawing. "I've seen this one before. It was with Vectus! Something about this dragon feels pure evil. Perhaps Vectus himself has poisoned the beast against its natural ways. Dragons are not hateful or evil by nature." he stated. Myra turned and looked at him, eyebrows raised. "Spoken like a true expert. Well done. It's true. Dragons are not evil by nature. They will defend themselves and others if necessary, or provoked. But an attack for sake of the attack would be impossible." Still looking at the black dragon, Jester spoke, "What if Vectus was able to, through some powerful magic, block the dragon's natural tendencies? Could it be done?" Myra looked directly at him, "Nothing is impossible when the dark powers are used. It would take someone of extreme evil intent, to exert that much power to a dragon and turn it against its own nature. It would require a continuous effort on the user of the dark powers to maintain that kind of control. The dragon would fight against the magic without ever giving up. A sad use of its energy." Myra looked down at the floor. It saddened her to think that such a majestic creature could be held against its will and forced to do the bidding of someone so evil. She sat in the chair next to him. She suddenly felt drained of her energy. "My knight, I must get some rest now or I'll be of no use to you at all. There is still much to discuss before you leave again. She stood and kissed him on the cheek and left for her bedchamber. Jester was numb with all that had transpired this night. He sat down and continued through the drawings of dragons. He went through the drawings carefully, a second time. For some reason, there was no 'Zara' dragon among them. He would have to ask Myra or Lord Dunvegan about her. Zara had fallen sleep on the table top. The evening's antics had taken their toll. Jester carefully reached across the table and gently placed his right hand on her head. Although she was asleep, she welcomed Jester to her thoughts. It was amazing to connect to another creature like this. No words were exchanged; it was like receiving a letter, delivered directly from one to the other. He was able to 'read' them in his mind. Zara too! Zara 'told' him they were growing and learning together. She was a small one, but capable of mastery of the sky. Her breed was one of the oldest in dragon memory. Her abilities as a dragon were growing daily now. She still needed more practice to fully develop her flying skills, but Tantrus was helping her along. She would need to spend more time with the great dragon in order to learn more of the dragon way. There was none of her kind anymore that she knew of. Myra and her father needed to help him with some of his new power. Its use would be required in the coming days. Time was running out. Both of our lives will be changed by this. Jester's vision blurred and he put his head down on the table for just a moment. He dreamt of dragons. Flying swiftly over the tree tops. Their fire burning everything, even stone heated beyond measure, exploding into pieces, unable to absorb any more heat. Dragon fire was a persistent thing.

Chapter Thirteen

(More than breakfast gets cooked)

He awoke with a start! He could smell ham and eggs cooking. A woman's voice, singing quietly, somewhere nearby. Zara was wrapped up in a scrolled drawing, with her eyes shut tight. The sunlight streamed through a window behind him. He was stiff from his sleep in the chair but felt ravenous with the smells of a morning meal. He slowly got up from the chair and stretched. His right leg was pins and needles. With a slight limp, he made his way to the cooking area of the pantry. She was bent over looking on a low shelf for something with her back to him. He quietly moved behind her and grabbed her by the waist. He was quickly grabbed behind the right knee and pulled off balance and fell heavily backwards onto the floor. Another moment and a cutting knife was at his throat. It was Shandahr! Jester was surprised and impressed by her quick action to render him helpless in a single blink of the eye. She recognised him and dropped the knife, then helped him to his feet again. "Jester! What on earth were you…" she stopped. "I'm sorry, I wasn't expecting that. Are you alright? Myra is still upstairs asleep! I was making something for you to eat. You must be hungry." Jester had both hands on his backside. It had been many years since he had been taken down that hard and fast by any one, man or woman. "It is I who owes an apology. I thought you were, well, yes, I'm starving! It smells wonderful." Shandahr laughed, "Well then, clear some room at the table. It will be ready soon." Jester tried very hard not to limp as he headed for the table, littered with drawings and a still sleeping Zara. As he was gently removing Zara from the drawing of the black two headed beast, Myra appeared at the bottom of the stairs. "Good morning to you. It smells so good in here. Did you sleep at all?" she asked. "Some, I think. I hope you're hungry" he said. Shandahr appeared from the pantry with a large platter of ham, eggs, and a strong smelling tea. The three of them sat and ate in silence. Zara went to the door and 'trilled' to be let out. Shandahr got up and let her out. Tantrus was awake and sniffed at Zara as she ran past to the grass. Momentarily, Zara returned and 'trilled' at Tantrus. The two dragons sat facing each other as if having a conversation. Shortly, Zara jumped and flew onto Tantrus's neck. The great dragon spread her wings and with a great rush of air, lifted off the courtyard stones and

into the sky. Little Zara clung tightly as the manor house
became smaller and smaller. Her eye's sparkled with
excitement! The countryside stretched out below in all
directions. Zara could see the great forest to the west, the
rocky hill top with the burnt circle below, and a glimpse
of the sea to the north. The eastern part of the kingdom
was obscured by low cloud cover. The great dragon
levelled off finally and started a slow roll to the left. Zara
knew it was time to let go. She spread her wings and
released her grip on Tantrus. She was able to maintain her
height with the adult dragon. Zara loved the feeling of
gliding high above the ground. They were high and far
enough to not be able to see the manor house clearly. They
continued their course northwards, towards the sea. Zara
could already smell the salt air as they neared the
coastline. Within a short while they were over the water.
The white lines of the waves were far below them. There
was a mist further out to sea that obscured her vision of
the horizon. Tantrus began a shallow dive, descending
towards the rough sea. Zara was able to keep up with little
effort. It was her first true flight and she loved the feeling
of the air against her. The smell of the salt water was
getting stronger now as they neared the water. The two
had descended below the mist and could see the rough
waters as far as the horizon now. They levelled off some
fifty feet above the surface and continued flying north.
The heavy dense air made the flight easier as the lift

generated by their wings was considerably more than at high altitudes. The moist air allowed short contrails from their wing tips and tails as they hurtled over the water. Zara was finally in her element. She knew she was born to fly. Tantrus glanced backward to check on Zara and let loose a great ball of white hot flame into the waters below them. Zara punched a hole through the column of steam created by the boiled water. She pulled up hard and rolled over and burst through the steam cloud a second time, then banked hard to the right and closed the gap between her and Tantrus. Her speed was near that of a bolt from a longbow. The water below was merely a blur. She managed to catch up to Tantrus and even passed her momentarily. She adjusted her wing angle and slowed somewhat. The larger dragon overtook her and continued northwards. Zara looked behind her briefly; they were well past all sight of land. Her natural compass allowed her to maintain a fairly straight line course along with the larger dragon. Tantrus suddenly dipped downwards and was just inches above the water now. She adjusted her direction slightly and snatched a large fish out of the water with her powerful rear legs, then climbed upwards and ate the fish. Zara tried to do the same. However, she grabbed a too large fish in her jaws, not her rear legs. With a foamy splash, she ended up on her back in the waves. She released the stunned fish as she gagged on the salt water. A very unpleasant taste for her. With a flutter of wings she was able to get clear of the water and spiral upwards again. Tantrus had circled her twice till she was clear of the water. The sea held creatures more than capable of eating Zara in a single bite. The two dragons regrouped and began a slow turn southwards. As the horizon changed from north to west, the dragons spotted many ships in the distance. There were hundreds of them fanned out in a wide arc. Both dragons knew this was the invasion force that the humans spoke of. Tantrus flew close to Zara and touched her gently with her wing tip. They both separated, Tantrus to the west, Zara hurtled east. At a point where the ships were barely visible, both dragons turned north again. When the ships were just behind them, they turned again. They flew towards each other at very high speed, just skimming the waters surface. As their distance closed they turned again towards the fleet of ships. Tantrus side-slipped towards Zara and again touched her wingtip on Zara. As they came up on the rear line of ships, both dragons dropped to just inches above the water. Their speed made the water appear flatter and without any detail. They shot between the ships in seconds, raking the black hulls with a blue flame. Then climbed and turned sharply for a second pass. This time head on. They changed the angle through the ships on this pass. In moments they were through and turning sharply for a final run between the dark hulls. A new direction again and past the blurred shapes! As the high speed pass was

completed, both dragons began to gain altitude quickly
before turning again for home. Both dragons had set fire
to nearly 200 ships. The fire was a very hot blue mixed
with some faint yellow flame. It was the highest heat range
a dragon could produce. Hard to see but it was
devastating. No amount of water could extinguish it. The
first ship to sink would burn, even underwater, all the way
to the bottom! Dragon fire is a persistent thing. The pair
of dragons made haste for the manor. Climbing to get
above the mist and cloud cover, so as not to be seen. A
greasy black smoke roiled into the sky far behind them.
Soon the pair began a slow descent through the broken
cloud. The manor house was far below. They turned in
unison and began a steep, short final approach to the
courtyard. Tantrus was a very accomplished flyer. She
began to let her powerful wings droop somewhat to create
drag and slow her descent. As she passed low, over the
manor's roof top she banked hard to the left as always.
Both wings raised quite high to spill even more air. Her
rear legs moved far forward in anticipation of the landing.
Once clear of the wall, she allowed all the air to spill from
under her wings and was on the ground. Zara had been
flying for hours now and was tired. She was also very new
at this and tried hard to copy what Tantrus had just done.
She was still too high, and unsure of the side-slip
manoeuvre Tantrus had used earlier. Her option was to
increase her downwards angle, but she gained speed as she

lost height. She aimed for a point just over the peak of the manor's slate roof. Her speed at this point was faster than any arrow could fly. She began to pull up out of the dive but sank below the roof line. The front of the manor grew very large, very fast. It was a solid wall of stone and many glass windows. In side the manor, Myra, Shandahr and Jester were about to begin dinner. The women had cooked a good sized wild turkey and were about to carve the bird. The table was beautiful. All the place settings were neatly arranged, and the center piece was the turkey, fresh from the oven. The three of them were seated at the table. Shandahr was facing the front of the manor. She looked out the window as Tantrus landed on the cobblestones outside. A moment later she noticed Zara, a small green shape, rocketing directly towards the window behind Jester. She opened her mouth wide to give warning but it was already was too late! The window exploded as Zara entered the manor's dining room. In a heartbeat Zara hit Jester in the back of his head, slamming him head first into the large bowl of cooked potatoes. Then hit the turkey head first. She was buried into the bird like an arrow. Her mass and speed however were not quite zeroed. The turkey, with Zara deeply embedded, hit Shandahr mid chest and she crashed backwards onto the floor. The turkey with its dragon stuffing slid a few feet further into the room before stopping.

125

It looked like a good sized troop of soldiers had ransacked the dinning room. Glass all over the floor, Jester wiping potato from his face, and Shandahr on the floor covered in the displaced stuffing from Zara's sudden entry into the bird's ribcage. The turkey made a strange 'trilling' sound and wobbled in a slow circle just past her head. Myra was speechless. She stood, holding her hands to either side of her head in utter disbelief! Tantrus came to the gaping hole that the window glass once occupied and looked in at the devastation. Zara struggled to free herself from the turkey. Both of her rear legs braced against the drumsticks.

Chapter Fourteen

(The beach and the field)

The dragons attack on the ships had been devastating. Out of nearly three hundred some odd ships, less than one hundred remained. They managed to rescue only ninety soldiers from the burning and sinking ships. Half of them would be unable to fight when landfall was made, within a day or two, depending on the winds. Although it was the first wave of the invasion, their plans would need to be radically altered to have any effect at all. Any surprise in their arrival was now lost. They would meet serious resistance. Each remaining ship posted look outs in-case the dragons returned. The captain of the advance invasion party ordered all the remaining ships to begin a slow turn back the way they had come. They would wait for the main fleet to arrive, before making landfall.

Back in Ionicus, the final wave of ships sailed from the harbour. Vectus, was among the many. He had no idea as of yet, that his first 'wave' of the invasion force had been crippled badly. They had a favourable wind and they set sail for Tyde. Within five days the invasion would begin in earnest! Vectus retired to his rear cabin to go over the maps again. Tyde would be his this time. Even though only a few of the advance scouts returned, he felt he had enough information to overpower any forces Tyde had to offer in its defence. His plan was to take it within a year. He had better troops, better trained, and his personal powers were at their peak. His two headed dragon sealed below decks, would wait till landfall was made till he unleashed its terrifying power!

In Tyde, things were getting ready for the 'reception'. Massive long bows, mounted in the sand, capable of launching a bolt far out to sea, lined the shores for miles. The bolts they would launch would easily compromise a ships hull, the fact they would be on fire when launched, would nearly destroy any ship they hit. The invasion force had much to worry about. The beach areas were covered in snare wires. Easily entangling a hapless soldier, the more he struggles, the more damage is done. The steep embankments from the shore to the mainland were set with huge logs, piled up so they can be rolled down hill into the enemy. A single swipe of a broadsword would be all that was needed to create mayhem down below on the rough gravel beaches! Finally, troops were stationed at regular intervals along the shores, more than enough to man the giant long bows and other entrapments.

Myra, Jester, and Shandahr had the terrible mess cleaned up in the manor house. Jester would send a glazier to the manor in a few days to replace the shattered window. Zara had been extracted from the turkey without issue. She was no worse for wear. Zara new now what she was borne for. The sky was her element. She needed practice for sure, but she was very fast, and very little for a dragon, both great attributes according to Tantrus. One day soon she would be a master of flight, and be one with the skies! Her diminutive size belied her very powerful abilities. Great things come from small packages! As things were, she loved Jester. He was her human mentor and she would remain with him as long as either lived. As a human, he made her feel loved, safe, and let her be herself. They had a real connection that would grow large in the weeks to come. Time was running out here, a great evil was fast approaching. Zara and her kind would play a major role in the outcome of the invasion of a few days hence. Jester needed to be ready with his new knowledge. Tantrus had alerted her to the fact many more dragons needed to be awakened. She knew there were many others waiting their turn for life and freedom. Left abandoned in nests for too long, they awaited the magic of dragon fire to bring them into the fold. Tantrus and Zara had a new mission over the next several days! Many dragons were needed quickly. They would begin a search and birth operation that might last a few days. Their survival may depend on it! They would leave in the predawn tomorrow. The kingdom would have many dragons again. Its existence depended on it now, more than ever!

Myra and Jester mounted their horses and left the courtyard. They were meeting Lord Dunvegan again. Much planning and further discovery waited. As they approached Dunvegan manor, they could see her father's soldiers leaving on a patrol of his lands. All wore their battle armour now. The sergeant at arms offered a stiff salute to the pair as they entered the large courtyard. Four guards were on duty at the main entry to the Manor. They politely stood aside as the two entered. "Come, be quick!" shouted Lord Dunvegan, from the library. He was standing at the large window looking upwards. He waved them over to the open window. "You must see this. It's been years since I've witnessed this!" he said excitedly. At first, they were unsure of what they should be looking at. Suddenly, Tantrus with Zara at her wingtip streaked across the sky, disappearing over the tree tops. They reappeared as they shot straight up. Both dragons rolled in opposite directions during their fast climb, then levelled themselves and began a swift dive straight at the manor. They blasted past the library wall at great speed. Several drawings blew off the desk as a rush of air rattled the windows. Jester cleared his throat. "Yes, some flight lessons are certainly in order for Zara." Both he and Myra laughed. "Please, be seated. May I offer either of you a drink?" asked Dunvegan. Myra nodded. "Why thank you, I believe we will." Jester removed his sword and scabbard and placed them by the door. Dunvegan poured the drinks. Jester picked up a goblet and raised it to Myra and her father. "May this evening be a great learning experience for us all." They drank to that. Dunvegan regarded Jester a moment. "Of that, my young friend, I can assure you! Lets get started shall we? As you know, time is of the essence now. Jester, how comfortable are you with Tantrus?" "Well sir, I feel safe with her, although still a sense of awe in her presence." he said. "Excellent! What about the company of many more dragons. Some even perhaps much larger than Tantrus?" Jester's eyebrows rose slightly. "Well, I can't really say sir. How many more dragons are we talking about here? I didn't think there were more than a handful left these days." he said. Sadly that was the truth now. During the battle with Ionicus years before, many dragons died. The nests were either destroyed or abandoned by the adults for their own safety. Food was scarce during and immediately after the Great

War due to the burning of farmlands by Vectus. Not to mention the extreme cold and snow that followed his departure. Most if not all the little ones died from it. Some dragons managed a meagre food supply and shelter, but could not reproduce. It was a combination of a lack of a mate, and a survival instinct. Dunvegan coughed, "The tables are to be turned again. A call to arms, as it were, is needed now. Finish your drinks and follow me please." Jester and Myra stood. They followed her father out through the rear exit where they had gone the day of the funeral. They crossed the field to the corner of the crumbling wall to a large partly sunken stone. It looked as if it had stood upright once. I was not just some random stone either. It was carved long ago. An ancient writing was discernable on its smooth surface. "This is a 'Dragon Stone'. One of three, in the entire kingdom. Only four people still living know of them and what they are used for. You are about to become the fifth." Jester could now sense a power within the stone. A feeling very similar to touching the two dragons during the transfers. "I know these stones" said Jester. "There is another not far from my castle. It's in the clearing, where I first met Myra. Zara's egg was beside it when I rescued it." Dunvegan put a hand on Jester's shoulder. "The stone must be righted again to point straight upwards. Myra?" She joined hands with her father and they bowed their heads together. They whispered words he did not understand, but seemed somehow familiar to him. The feel from the massive stone seemed to grow within him. He wanted to step back further but could not move. The ground around the base of the stone began to move. The heavy sod made a faint tearing sound as the stone began to right itself. The ground vibrated under his feet as the stone finally became fully upright. Myra and her father turned to look at the stone. The years of moss and lichen began to fall from the stone. It was renewing itself before his eyes. It looked as it must have when first placed there, centuries ago. Jester looked at Myra and her father, who both nodded at him. He stepped forward and placed both hands firmly on the smooth, cool stone. The same vision of the night before came back to him. He was engulfed in dragon fire. Not burning him at all. He raised his hand and held it high above his head. It felt like his very soul was emanating outwards through the stone. A moment later, Myra and Lord Dunvegan joined him at the stone. They too, placed their hands firmly on the stone. Momentarily, a ray of what looked like sunlight emanated from the top of the stone. It changed from a narrow beam of light pointing straight up, to a very wide arc, going horizontally in all directions. The three of them stepped back from the stone and looked up at the bright light radiating outwards. The property was lit in a strange glow. The sun had already set, but the area was illuminated by the stone's light. Jester could clearly see the field they stood in. Lord Dunvegan turned to face Jester. "Observe and learn" he stated simply. In another moment a great rush of air flattened the grasses as Tantrus landed next to them. Myra went over to her and rubbed her jaw line with her hand. Shortly, Zara landed nearby, a clod of dirt turning over as she did so. Jester smiled at that, almost there little one, he thought. Zara came over to him and sat watching the empty field. Presently a rush of air overhead announced another dragon was present. Jester's heart skipped a beat. He felt Myra's hand in his. He turned his head and looked at her. She smiled back and squeezed his hand. With its great wings raised and spilling air, a third large dragon landed nearby. It was as large as Tantrus, but a male. It snorted and clawed at the earth, then approached them, head lowered in a dragon bow of sorts. Tantrus exhaled loudly and bowed her head as well. Zara trilled loudly, startling Jester. Myra held his hand a little tighter. The stranger touched noses with Tantrus and Zara. Without any thought or prodding, Jester stepped forward and rubbed the dragon's lower jaw firmly, while placing his other hand on its head. The dragon welcomed his touch and settled down on its belly. Soon another and another dragon came to the field and the greeting was repeated in turn. Within a short while, fully eleven new dragons occupied the field. They were very tolerant of each other and seemed to be comfortable with the gathering. Jester was in total awe of the many variants of the creatures. One pony sized, another very elongated and thin, yet another that was almost all wings and no dragon. It was an amazing sight. The stone's light continued to radiate outwards. Little Zara came with Jester and greeted each dragon with him. It was if Zara already knew the dragons gathered here. Suddenly, a very powerful blast of air rolled across the entire field. It almost knocked Jester and Zara over by its sheer strength. The other dragons dug their claws in to the ground to maintain their position. The ground shook and trembled as something very heavy landed in the far corner of the field. The light on the stone went out abruptly. It was pitch black. Something very large indeed began moving towards them. The ground vibrated with each step. Jester noticed all the other dragons had placed their heads on the grass. Except Zara. She trilled loudly and ran off into the darkened field. Jester wished for a large torch suddenly. He put his hand to his swords handle but the sword was in the library, near the door. Myra came and stood beside him and put an arm around him. "Remember my father's words" she whispered. Lord Dunvegan came over and stood with them. He said a few strange words aloud and held up his hand over his head. The field was illuminated with a dull glow again. All Jester could see were four very powerful looking legs. He looked over at Myra and Dunvegan. They were looking almost straight up. Slowly he followed their gaze. Towering high above them was what had to be the largest dragon in the kingdom, likely the world. Something was moving on its head! He strained to see more detail. The giant head slowly lowered into the light. It was Zara! He felt Myra push him gently in the small of his back. He took a step forward. His knees shook. The gigantic head lowered down till even with Jester. Zara's eyes shone brightly back and she trilled in delight. Jester reached out and rubbed the massive jaw of the dragon. He willed his hand not to shake as he did so. He placed his other hand on the head, just in front of its right eye. He immediately felt calmed. The huge dragon let him know he had nothing to fear in him. The ground vibrated again as it settled onto the ground. A friendly spirit in such a gigantic body. Jester relaxed noticeably. Dunvegan came up to Jester and said, "We know this dragon as 'King'. Don't let his size fool you. Next to Zara, he is the youngest dragon here." "And so you shall remain 'King'" said Jester to no one in particular. "There is one more task ahead tonight, young man. Assemble the dragons if you please." Zara jumped from 'King's' head onto her place on Jester's shoulder. Jester was surprised at himself. Somehow, he knew what he needed to do. He turned and faced the other dragons. They all came forwards and made a complete circle around him. He was surrounded by dragon noses. He knelt down with them on the grass. Then, ran his right hand across all the noses. Sleep, he thought. Before dawn you will search out the all the eggs of the departed dragons and bring them here. Tomorrow at sunset, the great awakening will begin. It was a thought he transferred. No actual words, as such. He stood. Zara trilled loudly and spread her wings, blocking his sight briefly. He lifted Zara off his shoulder and placed her on the ground. He headed back to the manor with Myra and her father. "You have done well. I'm most impressed with you." said Myra. Lord Dunvegan looked Jester in the eye. "You now realize young man, you are the Dragon Master. They are all connected to you now. They know the game plan from you and trust in you. As I knew they would accept you. Well done!" "What if they hadn't accepted me?" asked Jester. "There would be precious little of you to send home." said Dunvegan.

Chapter Fifteen

(Day of the dragons)

The night sky was about to change into dawn, as it had since time began. The dragons stood and stretched their wings to full height. It would be a day of flying and searching. Something dragons loved to do. Except it was not food they were looking for. Jester had begun an ancient call they must all heed. The oldest dragon among them had done this only twice before in its lifetime. The dragons departed the field in all directions. They flew low and slow over treetops, and open ground. Some followed the rivers and shorelines. The search had begun in earnest.

It was midday when the first dragon returned to the field behind Dunvegan Manor. It landed gracefully in the soft earth and sat back. Lowering its head to just above the grass, it regurgitated up fully five 'stones' onto the ground. Carefully, it rolled them into a cluster on the ground. Satisfied with the arrangement, it turned into the wind and left again. As it departed the field, several others made a low pass over the field and turned to land. The groupings of 'stones' continued all day long. Eventually the massive dragon known as 'King' approached the manor and landed heavily in the field. He lowered his great head to near ground level and coughed. His jaws were open wide. A single tiny stone rolled off his tongue into the grass! It was a little smaller than Zara's egg had been. Pleased with the delivery, 'King' departed the field in search of more.

Jester and Myra returned to the field in the late afternoon. Jester was speechless. Eggs occupied the entire field. The dragons were using the adjacent field now. Zara had remained with Jester and Myra. Her size was not suited to carrying the heavy eggs. She was very excited and ran off into the clusters, trilling again and again. "There is something in the field that is attracting her." said Myra. Zara bounded through the grass till she came to the smallest egg. She trilled in delight and made several smoke rings! Jester and Myra approached and froze on the spot. The egg was nearly identical to Zara's egg. "I think I need another bear rug!" said Jester. Myra laughed. "I think you might! It really could be a Zara sibling!" "I need to ask your father about Zara, she just can't be the only one of her kind." stated Jester. He kneeled in the grass and touched the egg. "Yes, it's another Zara, but a male." He looked up at Myra. "When can the hatching begin?" "It already has." she pointed to Zara. She had made a smoke ring that surrounded the egg and waited for Jester to move back a little. The ring ignited with a bright yellow flame, then turned more bluish in colour. Although the heat was intense, most of it was directed at the egg. Zara repeated the smoke ring. It ignited with a pure blue flame. It was more a brief flash, than the first ring. Zara went up to the egg and seemed to listen, her head tilting beside it. Jester and Myra watched closely. The egg rocked a little. Zara trilled loudly and looked at them, eyes sparkling with excitement.

More and more eggs arrived during the day. Jester had several groups of eggs ready to hatch. Tantrus and Zara began the process of the 'birthing fire'. Most eggs began to hatch shortly after the ritual. Lord Dunvegan's men were busy with numerous grass fires but managed to keep them to a minimum. Zara kept running back to 'her' egg. It did the same wild rolling motions as hers had. Several times Jester and Myra had to jump high to let it pass, or dart off to the side. The 'wild' egg finally stopped at the dragon stone after a resounding head on crash. It split open, and Zara's slightly smaller twin trilled its first sound. Jester and Myra gathered the hatchlings over to one side of the field, like a nursery of sorts. Food of every kind was brought to them by Dunvegan's men. There were over ninety hatchlings in the field now, with more to come. Jester was very pleased with how things progressed but was filled with doubts about how they would be of much help against Vectus. Lord Dunvegan joined them amid the trilling, growling, clamouring hatchlings. "Your army grows dragon master! A very good start I'd say." He laughed. "Sir, I can't help but think how long they need to grow up some, prior to the invasion force making landfall. We have days at best!" said Jester. "I have sent a dragon to check on their progress. We will know soon how long we have!" said Dunvegan. "After the damage Tantrus and Zara inflicted a few days ago, Vectus will be extremely careful where, and more importantly, when, he makes landfall. We are ready for him this time, no surprises." Dunvegan smiled almost imperceptivity. "I'm not so sure a horde of dragon babies are going to offer much resistance to Vectus. Unless he laughs himself to oblivion, we still have a big problem." Jester looked at the ground. Dunvegan put his hand on his shoulder. "Jester, you are the dragon master, what would you do?" "They need training, knowle… Yes, you're right! Of course!" Jester was on his game now. He closed his eyes and asked the dragons to form a large circle. In a moment they had formed a circle. A few of the older adult dragons joined as well. The learning had begun. The dragons began communicating with each other. It was much like a collective knowledge. Each dragon learned of the impending invasion and what would be expected of them. Individual abilities would be shared and ways to enhance them brought forward. Other than food and some rest, the hatchlings would begin training tomorrow. The 'teaching' would go on throughout the night.

Dusk was fast approaching as the last of the adults returned with their cargo of 'found' eggs. Jester was amazed at how many eggs had been collected. He had lost count midday, as so many covered the ground in two fields. Tantrus and Zara had been assigned the birthing fires duties and most eggs had hatched. Some, like the 'Zara' egg would take somewhat longer to finally hatch a dragon baby. All eyes turned west, as 'King' flew over the fields. His tail was low and he laboured to remain airborne. After a very awkward and heavier than usual landing, he was able to regurgitate a large pile of some 30 'Zara' eggs! He had discovered several nests buried long ago, deep within the forest. His gigantic size allowed him to carry all of the eggs in a single load. A look of relief, for a dragon, washed over him as the last egg was disgorged into the grass. Zara was beside herself with excitement! Jester shook his head. "This is a turning point for us. They will definitely make a difference to the next step." He said to Myra and her father. Dunvegan regarded Jester. "I agree. Things are looking up here. There are, however, many more to be added to the roster." Jester looked at Dunvegan with raised eyebrows. "Young man, you still have much to learn, follow me please." They went to the manor and entered the main hall. His sergeants at arms, along with a dozen of his men were waiting in the hall. Dunvegan strode to the center of the room. The floor had a large carpet of finely woven course fibres with many small squares in a diagonal pattern from one corner to the other. He bent down, and felt along one of the squares, then peeled the carpet back to reveal a large door in the floor. Dunvegan pushed downwards with his foot and the door slowly opened, revealing steps leading down below. The sergeant lit a small lantern and handed it to him. He and Jester descended the steps into a large room under the floor of the main hall. Inside the hidden room were many dozens of eggs, similar to the Zara eggs! It was a treasure trove of eggs, all neatly lined up on the many shelves. "I have been the keeper of the eggs, since the last great war! Zara will have many companions this time around!" said Dunvegan. His men assembled and began to carry the eggs up to the field above. Zara would be beside herself with brothers and sisters! Truly a night for the dragons of Tyde! "I wanted to tell you since we first met. It would not have made sense then, but now I think it does! We still have much to do." Dunvegan gestured at the stairs. "Shall we?" They ascended to steps back to the main hall. Jester and Dunvegan sat at a small table near the doors. "It is time I tell you about your Zara. She was, we thought, the last of her kind to be hatched. Zara is one of the ancient dragons. A true master of the skies. They are the fastest fliers, and can produce the hottest flame of any dragon known. This breed of dragon was instrumental in the defeat of Vectus and his black dragons during the last of the Great War. Their small size is no indication of their power as a dragon. They were the first breed to seek out certain humans and attempt to bond with them. Their intelligence is truly amazing. We are not alone in this world with the ability to reason and learn new things. Zara's egg was found partway up the stony hill, behind Myra's house. She decided to let Tantrus hatch the egg near the first dragon stone. Its power is greater than the one here. It obviously worked!" Dunvegan smiled at Jester. "We better check on Myra and see how the brood is fairing eh?" They headed out to where Myra was watching the circles of dragons. The 'Zara' eggs were about to be hatched momentarily. Zara had her first 'brother' with her and Myra. Tantrus and King had also joined them. The three of them would create the hatching fire to begin the birthing. Everyone left the area, except Jester. The dragons had 'asked' him to remain with them. Jester's heart raced in the anticipation. He looked over his shoulder back at Myra, her father, and his men. All of whom were at a safe distance away. Jester picked up Zara and placed her on his right shoulder. She 'trilled', and the three of them each sent a large, dense, smoke ring out over the carefully arranged eggs. All three rings floated one above the other, surrounding the immediate area. On cue, the triple rings burst into wild flames of three differing colours. Although Jester knew the flame would not harm him, the heat was still noticeably intense. Dragon fire was a persistent thing. The eggs went from a stone grey to a dull red colour that seemed to brighten with every passing moment. The flames themselves were also very dense. Jester could not see the far side of the ring through the flames. Zara made a final smoke ring that circled the group. It ignited in a brilliant blue flash. The flames disappeared and the eggs were nearly white from the heat. As quickly as it had begun, the eggs began the process of cooling off. Many more dragons would enter this night in Tyde.

Jester placed Zara back on the ground. Already some of the eggs had begun shedding bits of the outer shell. This was the quickest he'd ever seen this particular dragon egg begin the hatching process. Previous experience told him it was time to move away from the eggs now. This part of the field would become very active soon! He made his way over to Myra and her father. Myra took his hand. "I think it's time for a grand supper. Shandahr has been busy most of the day preparing the meal for tonight. We have a few guests tonight." "I don't recall seeing anyone arrive tonight." said Dunvegan. "Well we have several very important guests tonight, including one you haven't seen in many years. You have been too busy organizing the hatchings with Jester. I'm not at all surprised either of you not having noticed the Kings horses in the courtyard." Jester and Dunvegan looked at each other, and then looked towards the courtyard. A group of the King's horses stood patiently as well as a few from his own castle. His sergeant would be here too! The three of them headed for the manor house.

The King himself was there, surrounded by several of his squires and his sergeant at arms. Jester, Myra, and Dunvegan all bowed deeply to the King. Dunvegan was nearly speechless. "My King, I'm honoured to have your presence in my humble home. To what do I owe this special occasion?" he stammered. "Lord Dunvegan, it is I who must confess to you my uncertainty of things from our past. I beg your forgiveness in those matters. You have rallied what I believe to be a new, but formidable army. You are well founded in your trust and faith of Jester. I had hoped of great things to come from his corner of the kingdom. It appears that between the two of you, things are well in hand. As far as we know, Vectus is just off our shores but keeping his distance for the time being. He must know we have a welcoming planned for him and his kind." said the King. There was quiet laughter around the main hall. "I cannot tell you how grateful we are to have

your combined and extensive knowledge of dragons on
our side. We would all like to forget the last Great War,
but this new invasion will not go as Vectus has planned
it would. Your lovely daughter Shandahr has filled us in
on the events thus far." The King coughed and cleared his
throat. "My sword please!" he commanded to no one in
particular. A squire handed him his sword. It was a very
old broadsword. It shone like it had the day it was made.
Jester was surprised to notice the crest was identical to
his sword. The King held it point up. "Lord Dunvegan,
please kneel before me." Dunvegan looked at Jester, who
raised his eyebrows slightly and winked at him. The
king placed his sword flat side down on Dunvegan's left
shoulder. "By my power of King, sovereign ruler of Tyde, I
hear by bequeath you as a knight of the realm." The King
now placed the blade onto Dunvegan's right shoulder.
"From this night hence, you shall be a knight of Tyde.
Your power of command shall be yours with my blessing
always. You are sworn to protect the kingdom, your
people, and family from this night forth, till unable to do
so in your last breath." The sword moved to just above his
head now. "All hail Sir Dunvegan, Knight of Tyde! You
may now rise Sir Knight!" Everyone cheered and clapped.
Myra nodded at the waiting staff to bring the meal and
drinks. Dunvegan was stunned by what just happened.
Myra hugged him and congratulated him, as did Jester
and Shandahr. Ronald also came and touched his head to

his father. A sign of respect for him. Soon the meal and drinks were out of the pantry. It was a wonderful feast, but without the gaiety that would normally be present on such an occasion. A serious battle plan was to be formed by nights end.

The room was filled with many lit candles. The weak shadows seemed to vibrate from the many light sources in the room. Warming fires were set in the large fireplaces at either side of the manor's main hall. Jester thought it would have been interesting to have Tantrus on her perch high above them on the ceiling, but she was otherwise occupied with Zara and the hatchlings in the nearby field. The King had brought all his advisors, lords and emissaries from all over the kingdom. Jester had a chance to catch up on things with his own sergeant. The castle was in full readiness for battle. Even the trap door over the moat was well oiled and back in service again. He made a personal note of that. Everyone who was unable to defend themselves, were now safely behind his castle walls. All sentries were on the lookout for dragons or troops, not of their own. The armoury was almost empty now. All beachhead positions were fully manned as well throughout the kingdom. Special provisions were made to protect everyone from the enemy dragon fire. Shields made from dragon scales, and a new material made from tiles from his own armoury that would not absorb or transfer much

heat, were set up at all beachhead areas. They were as
ready as they could be.

The men at the huge tables in the main hall went
over their plans and many contingencies. Jester excused
himself along with Myra and 'Sir' Dunvegan to check on
the dragon's progress. "Jester, I don't know what to say
to this. A great honour, but somehow I feel unworthy of
this Knighthood bestowed upon me." said Dunvegan.
"Sir Dunvegan, it is a title to which you whole heartedly
deserve. It's more than a way for the King to forgive
you for a badly perceived situation. It's a long overdue
reward for all the many efforts you have contributed to
the kingdom overall! Well done Sir Knight!" Jester smiled
back at Dunvegan. "Personally, we would have been lost
and unawares yet again, if not for your direct effort, and
keen knowledge of things few others understand. I may
be dragon master now, but it's in no small thanks to you.
I still have much to learn from you. I hope we have time
to add to the momentum you have created!" Myra put her
arm around Jester and squeezed him close. "You know
there was a time I thought you were too good to be true?
It turns out you are more than good, and very true! The
road ahead will be dangerous, perhaps fatal to many. We
must keep our end goals in mind always. Vectus, for all
his dark magic, and heart of ice, is still mostly human and
can be defeated, perhaps even destroyed. Like all of us, I

wish to end the threat from Ionicus, once and for all." she stated.

The field was alive with dragons. Many circles of learning had been formed. The adults were teaching the young. Zara was with her same breed cousins. Jester could tell her apart from the others by her horns as she helped with the learning circle. Such dedication from the dragons to themselves and mankind was truly amazing. The new dragons practiced fire, and smoke rings. There was not a blade of grass near them, that didn't crunch to ash when stepped on. Jester, with Myra and Sir Dunvegan worked their way through the hatchlings, taking in the training and estimating their numbers.

Chapter Sixteen

(Invasions don't always go as planned)

Vectus was getting antsy with all the delays since leaving Ionicus. His second sailing finally met up with the first sailing. Well, what was left of it. He was dismayed at the losses from only two dragons, so his men had said. Impossible, he thought! The little green dragons had all died many years ago. He's seen to that himself. They sailed along the coast in both directions, looking for a suitable landing site for their invasion forces, but found no obvious opportunities. The delays were unacceptable, but nothing was open or available to form a beach head from which to mount a major attack on Tyde. His powers of the dark magic allowed him to see the preparations that had been made on the beaches. Tyde was in full readiness for him. His options had been taken away this time. He returned to his planning in his cabin below decks! Over a third of his invasion fleet had been sunk. Unbelievably, by just two dragons! Very fast moving, but one was reported as being very large. Someone was shielding the dragons from his abilities to 'see' what he was up against this time. Someone else, with the dark powers could do that. It was one of his only fears, finding another with similar powers. He tried with all his might to see beyond the shielding but was unable to break through. His only clear option was to unleash the two headed beast below decks. Let it go on a rampage, burn everything, then he would come ashore and finish what he started long ago. Tyde would indeed fall to its knees.

A shouting of men above deck broke his concentration. He came up on deck to see what was happening. In the distance, a lone dragon soared high above the water. It was moving slowly along the same course they currently sailed. Vectus glared at the dragon and forced his immense will towards it. Using the dark power, he pushed with all his might. He willed it to drop from the sky into the sea below. He willed it to drown in the salty waters. The dragon faltered and tumbled once, then again. It fell from the sky towards the water. Vectus smiled ever so slightly. His men cheered at the sure demise of the dragon. They all waited for the huge splash as the dragon hit the water. It never came. At the last possible moment it turned sharply and streaked towards Vectus's ship. Only inches above the wave tops, its speed created white contrails of water vapour from its massive wing tips. Its great speed allowed it to close on the ship at an alarming rate. The men ran in panic. Vectus held his place at the railing and continued to force his will on the dragon, now moments away. Suddenly the great dragon hit the water with tremendous force. It was just feet away. A gigantic wall of water erupted as it crashed heavily into the waves. Thousands of gallons of icy seawater cascaded down onto his ship. The water pounded onto the decks, smashing everything, the main sails, ripped from the masts, landed heavily over one side. The huge swell from the dragon's impact nearly rolled the ship onto its opposite side. Vectus was swept from the deck and down into the forward cabin's stairwell. A dozen men surged past him. He managed to grab onto a rope less cleat before he could be drowned below decks. As his ship began to right itself in the foamy seas, the dragon he thought now drowned, burst from the water on the opposite side of the ship. A searing blast of dragon flame hit the decks and masts. The deadly flame continued down the length of the ship. The dragon rose from the water and set fire to ten more of his ships, before turning away from the fleet, headed away and inland. Away from any power Vectus could apply to it. His ship was now engulfed in flames. Fully armoured men leapt into the waves by the hundreds. They and their doomed ships would burn all the way to the bottom. Vectus managed to throw him self overboard and grabbed hold of a large piece of wooden hatch covering. His ship listed heavily, its bow was close to being completely submerged. Vectus commanded the creature below decks to free itself. Moments later, the sea erupted again as the black as night two headed dragon leapt from the water. The iron chains that once held it below decks, now trailed out behind it. The creature flew in a wide lazy circle over the fleet. Vectus was picked up by another ship. He was almost in shock of what had just happened. A very powerful shield it was. He was suddenly angry. Whoever was behind this shielding must die. This was now the new plan. Kill the sheilder, take the kingdom!

That night, a lone longboat left the fleet for the rocky shores of Tyde. In it were four men. Vectus was among them, dressed in light armour that was common in Tyde. They had the grim task of sneaking past the shore defences and killing the person who had the dark powers. They could tell who had these powers, as they were known as see'ers. They could feel the power within the person responsible for the shield. They all pulled hard on their oars, Vectus would not take any prisoners this time. Failure was not an option.

They managed to get ashore among the dark rock outcroppings. They climbed the boulders and were able to walk inland past the beach defences without being questioned. They blended in with the other soldiers and made their way down the rows of giant longbows. Every tenth longbow had a large earthenware pot filled with a flammable tar, to light the bolts with. As Vectus passed each one, he turned it to a black watery substance that would not burn. The stockpiles of bolts, made from strong and straight wood were warped slightly by his magic. They would never fly true. Most would never even reach the waters edge. The wood from the great longbows themselves was weakened, thereby greatly reducing their range. After ruining several miles of defences, Vectus and his men headed inland in search of the other with the dark powers. Soon the invasion could get underway without further resistance. For good measure, he brought on a steadily thickening fog from the sea. By morning the visibility would be down to just a dozen yards.

Chapter Seventeen

(Good news, bad news)

Sir Dunvegan staggered but regained his balance. He seemed suddenly pale. Myra took his arm and steadied him, "Father, what is it? Are you ill?" she was deeply concerned. "It's the dragon. The scout I sent earlier. It's returning now. Vectus caused it to crash into the sea, its hurt. It will be here in a moment. You must see to its well being Myra!" Dunvegan sat heavily on the soft earth of the dragon's field. The familiar rushing of air from a dragon landing nearby ruffled the few remaining clumps of grass. The dragon had a damaged left wing and forward shoulder. It landed clumsily in the far field. Myra and Jester headed towards it. The beast had its left wing fully out-stretched on the ground. Myra knew it had been broken just past the mid wing joint. Its left forward shoulder had been dislocated as well. "I'm surprised it was able to continue flying after that happened" said Jester. Myra rubbed the dragon's lower jaw and placed her other hand on its head. "It's something we call will power. It didn't want to stay close to Vectus. His power may have overridden my father's shielding of it. At least, momentarily. This one will need help for awhile." Myra walked around to the damaged wing. She looked at Jester and said, "Hold the end of the wing still if you can." Jester picked up the wing end in both hands and steadied it as best he could. Myra knelt in front of the damaged area and placed her hands on either side of the leading edge, with the break in the middle. She bowed her head and closed her eyes. Slowly she moved her hands together over the break. The dragon's wing shook slightly and it exhaled loudly. Jester could feel a slight warmth spread into the wing tip. Momentarily, Myra stood and walked back to the shoulder. She placed her cheek against the shoulder and touched the dragon. It exhaled loudly again, then settled. Its eyes finally closed. She walked over to Jester, still holding the wing. "Its ok, gently lower it to the ground now. We have done what we can. It will heal, but not before the battle begins I'm afraid. I want her to remain still for as long as possible." Jester carefully placed the wing end onto the ground. "She set fire to the ship Vectus was on and ten others. She was lucky to survive his magic. My father is in grave danger. Vectus will have his vengeance. He has lost much on this invasion and it has yet to begin." "You mean he knows it's your father behind this?" asked Jester. "Not exactly who, but

I know he can sense the presence of another who holds the dark powers." Myra looked worried now. A rush of air overhead and Zara landed on Jester's right shoulder. She trilled in excitement and flapped her wings in Jester's face. Both he and Myra laughed. "Zara! Your powers of flight have improved immensely! Nice landing. You have been learning and practicing I see." Zara's eyes were on the hurt dragon now. She trilled again, and leapt to the ground. Carefully, she touched her nose to the sleeping dragon behind them. Jester wanted her to spread the knowledge of what happened with this dragon. If knowledge is power, more couldn't hurt. Jester looked at Myra. "We need to talk to your father, and the King." Jester said flatly.

The King and all the guests had almost finalized their planning when Jester and Myra returned to the main hall. The room went silent. "My King, we have further news of Vectus." said Jester. "Please, seat yourselves. Tell us what you know." stated the King. A page pulled up two chairs for them. "A dragon scout has just returned from the coast. Vectus is looking for an opening in the defence lines. The dragon managed to burn eleven more ships, one of which was his flagship." The room broke into cheering and applause. The King held his hand up and everyone quieted again. "All we have done is fill him with further resolve to attack us. He will make a move soon I think. Our dragons are still sharing collective knowledge and training. Another month or two would be great, but I think it's a matter of a few days, maybe less. I hope we have done everything we can. Vectus will be upon us soon." Jester placed both his hands on the table edge and looked at everyone in the room. "We will need every advantage we can put to use." The King stood. "Well said young man. You all heard him clearly. Return now to your lands, and ready yourselves. May our common sense, our dragons, and our fellow man prevail here. The gods, I'm trusting to commend our actions in that Tyde will prevail when this darkness is finally over!" The room burst into cheers and applause again. Outside in the courtyard the horses and coaches were ready for their departures.

Jester caught up with his sergeant. "Everything at full alert from here on in my friend. Ready a small troop of our best fighters and scouts. I'll meet you back here within the day!" said Jester. The sergeant looked down and shook his head sadly. "Sir, take a look in the clearing behind you." The sergeant winked at him. Jester turned and saw his men patiently waiting. The sergeant had known that Jester would want them by his side from here on. The sergeant cleared his throat. "I trust this was quick enough for you?" Jester rolled his eyes. "You know me well my friend. Have them set up a light camp. We may need to move out quickly. I'll meet you back here in the manor hall." The sergeant smiled and headed off towards the men. Jester entered the hall and said some farewells to the departing crowd. He then stopped at the library door and found Dunvegan alone at his desk. Drawings of dragons still covered its top. "Sir, if I might have a word?" he asked. "By all means Jester, make yourself at home. Can I offer you a drink?" "Thank you Sir, I believe I will." Dunvegan got up and poured two drinks. "Sir, I believe you are in great danger from Vectus. He knows someone is shielding the dragons and everything else they can from his powers. We had your scout come back with wing and shoulder damage. She managed to sink his flag ship and ten others before returning here. I think he may make an attempt on your life. It makes sense to be able to drop the shields. It would put the advantage back in his favour again. Would you consider moving temporarily to my castle for safe keeping?" Jester took a long drink of his ale. Dunvegan seemed to consider the offer. He walked to the window and looked out into the evening. The departing troops and dignitaries clattered and rumbled past on horseback and by carriage. He turned and regarded Jester. "You make a kind offer my friend. However, my place is here, in the manor. Consider me your assistant dragon master if you will. You also may need my expertise should anything happen untoward. Vectus knows someone is creating interference with his plans and his dark magic. He also knows it's some one of great skill. I should think he will be very cautious this time round. A mistake or blunder would cost him dearly. He is a human, but with out heart and soul. He relies on his powers entirely, unlike myself. That is his first mistake. I doubt he will underestimate things as before. If I were him, I'd seek out the sheilder, and destroy him. Perhaps it is an opportunity for ourselves to take him early on. I will remain with you till this thing is finished, as will Myra. I will however, ask that Shandahr and Ronald be allowed to stay at your castle. They both should be safer there." Dunvegan sat in his desk chair. "Of course, I'll have two of my men escort them this very night." said Jester. "Not required, I'll have several of my own men do the escort. I'd rather you have all your men available, seeing as you work so well together. The rest of my troops who are not manning beachfront weapons will remain here as we need them. I'll have a wide perimeter set from this moment on. The action can begin at any time I think." Both men stood and headed for the main hall. Both Dunvegan's and Jester's sergeants waited in the hall. Dunvegan began issuing orders to his own sergeant as they walked to the main entry. Jester and his sergeant sat at a table in the main hall. "I think we should be ready for anything at any time. Have we set up a messenger rider to go to the coast and back from here? Wait! I can use one of the dragons for that! Much faster, plus it frees up our troop for business as it comes to us. Sergeant? Any things we might have missed?" "Well sir, I'd send a couple of dragons now, for a report on our readiness. Otherwise, we wait for the anvil to drop." said the sergeant.

Jester and the sergeant headed out to the dragon's field. The sergeant was somewhat apprehensive as they walked among the many dragons. They soon came to the group of little ones that were like Zara. Of course Zara was with them and she trilled in delight as Jester and the sergeant approached. Zara immediately flew to Jester's right shoulder and perched there. The sergeant was not so lucky. Within seconds he had three dragons perched on him. One on each shoulder and one on his head. The sergeant froze and smiled numbly. Jester laughed, as he knew the sergeant was uncomfortable amidst the many dragons surrounding him. "Looks like you have made a friend or two I'd say. Lucky for you they have already imprinted on Zara and some with Tantrus. You're not in any danger my friend. In fact, you are likely the safest you'll ever be right now." laughed Jester. "Thanks, I'll remember that." said the sergeant. Jester placed his right hand on Zara's muzzle and communicated with her. Zara jumped into the group of dragons and touched noses with three others. A moment later, with a flutter of wings, they departed the field, heading towards the coast. "We will know very shortly how things are progressing on the beaches sergeant. Zara and her kind can see very well in the dark. I expect to know our current situation in a very short while. Can I help with your burden sergeant?" "Yes, I'd be very much indebted to you Jester if, you could assist me." said the sergeant firmly. Jester took the three dragons from the sergeant and placed them back on the ground. A look of relief washed over the sergeant. "Thank you for that. I have never had a dragon sit on me let alone three at once. How many of them are there? Looks like three hundred or better, I'd say." "Well, you're off, just slightly. At last count we were just over seven hundred of them. All breeds accounted for. There may be a few more since our tally of a few hours ago." Myra waded through the little dragons and gave Jester a smile and nodded at his sergeant. "Well, sergeant, I see you're busy making many new friends. Please, put yourself at rest. You have nothing to fear here tonight. At dawn, most will begin some advanced flying techniques. Most will sleep this night as tomorrow may bring the expected and not so expected. I'm glad you are here for Jester. I for one, will sleep better knowing that. Now, if you'll excuse me, I'm off for some sleep myself." said Myra. Jester held her briefly and kissed her neck. "Sleep well, while you can." he stated. "I'll see you both tomorrow for breakfast." she said, and left for the manor house. The sergeant cleared his throat. "Sir, if I may say so, I'd scatter the dragons tonight. Have them fly to various points in the kingdom so as to be ready for what may happen soon. I can't help but think if they are all in this one location, they'd be an easy target for

Vectus's magic. We will need them more than ever when
this thing gets started. Let's not put all the 'eggs' in a
single basket for what could become an Ionicus breakfast."
"Thank you for those words sergeant. An excellent idea."
Jester knelt down on one knee and touched his hand
to Zara's head. After a moment, he stood. Zara trilled
at him and the sergeant and then spread her wings and
flew to where Tantrus was resting. In a few moments,
several dozen hatchlings along with an adult dragon
left the field and headed further inland. In the next few
moments, more dragons departed the field. Jester turned
to his sergeant. "Have the men assemble in the manor
hall sergeant. There are a few things I'd like to chat with
them about." The sergeant turned and headed for the
encampment near the trees across from the courtyard.
Jester watched another wave of dragons fly past him into
the night. Soon the fields would be nearly empty. Zara,
with twenty of her siblings remained, along with Tantrus
and King.

The three dragons, led by Zara flew roughly south
towards the coast. Normally she would have done this
at a fairly high altitude. Tonight they flew low and slow.
Just above the tree tops at a leisurely pace. The dragons
could see the ground where it was open and the forest
canopy in fine detail. The half moon was bright this night
as they cruised towards the ocean. Soon they could smell

the cooking fires of the coastal troops as well as the salt air. Rather than fly a straight line, Zara had them very close together and a random zigzag flight line. Just in case someone wanted to take a shot as they went overhead. A constant turn left, then right, made them so much less a target. Their turn intervals were always changing too. A very difficult shot, plus the bonus of making the simple flight a little more interesting. A few moments later, the dragons burst from the forest canopy, over the beach, and began a wide slow turn over the ocean. They lined up parallel with the beach and slowed further to observe the troops as they went about their duties. After several miles of beach patrol, Zara headed straight south over the open ocean again. She kept very low to the water to avoid being spotted by anyone on the lookout for dragons. The air was very dense tonight and a fog was forming quickly off the waters surface. The dragon's vision was still sharp though. Soon a few dim lanterns from the Ionicus fleet could be seen. The ships were far enough away as to not be seen from land, but just barely. All the ships bows were pointed northward as they drifted on the tide, slowly closing the distance towards shore. The light breeze was perfect for an early morning landing. Zara wanted to burn several more ships that night. Give the others a taste of what they could do. As she was considering the possibilities, a dark shadow moved with them. It was slightly upwards and behind them. She knew instinctively it was another dragon.

There was a slight metallic ringing that accompanied the shadow. Definitely not one of their own. Zara eased forward with her speed, the three others kept up with her. The shadow began to fall back slightly. Zara touched wing tips with the other three and asked that they do exactly what she does. She suddenly snapped a very hard left turn, and accelerated to a very high speed. She hurtled towards the beach at an extreme velocity. The thickening fog hid the contrails forming off their wingtips. The three new dragons were at their maximum speed, or so they thought. The shadowy dragon behind them had turned hard as well, but its sheer size and mass, prevented it from turning as quickly as the three little ones had. The shadow dragon climbed slightly to re-acquire its intended prey. Zara dropped down just over the waters surface. The beach was approaching at a very high rate of speed. Zara knew the area well and guided her two new scouts into the forest, well below the canopy this time. They bled off their speed, slowing to accommodate the forest trail. A moment later they were on the ground. They scurried into the dense underbrush. Zara looked upwards in time to see the huge black bodied dragon arc overhead. She shook slightly as the realization dawned on her. The black dragon that pursued them had two heads. Next to Zara's kind, they were extremely rare, and very deadly. This was a dragon that could not easily be caught by surprise. Zara noted the lengths of chain trailing out from behind its four legs. The black dragon had passed over Zara and her new scouts unawares of their exact location. The three dragons were about to leave the underbrush when four very silent men walked noiselessly past them on the trail towards Dunvegan's manor. They wore the usual armour all the local troops had but spoke not a word. In Tyde, the troops always had something to discuss or sing about. The invasion had not yet begun. There was no reason so far, to be so quiet. One man in the group was extremely tall. He moved with a steady grace but was very guarded. Their skin was very dark as well. Perhaps it was from being on the beach for days during the preparations. All of Tyde's troops used the traditional broadsword, these men carried crossbows. The kind she had burned when she and Jester had taken the Ionicus scouts prisoner. Zara knew something with them didn't fit. After a safe waiting period, the three dragons emerged onto the trail. Zara touched the other three with her nose briefly. They would fly at speed about 20 feet above the trail. As they overtook the four men they would each use a light flame to get their attention. The idea was to burn the crossbows and the spare bolts. It would be a high speed pass only, no turning back. If they could shed their armour fast enough, they would survive the attack with minimal burns but loose any firepower they may have to bear. They shot over the trail at a good speed, all the dragons in a very close formation. They rounded a gentle curve in the trail and were upon the four soldiers. The dragons each shot a yellowish flame on to the four men and accelerated away.

Vectus dropped as the first flames hit them. He rolled quickly off the trail into the dense underbrush. His three men were not quite as fast and dropped their weapons and screamed out in their native tongue. Two of the three men were able to discard their amour and suffered minor burns. The fourth man was not so lucky and dropped face down onto the trail. The dragon fire had continued to burn through the armour and soon he lay still. Vectus was furious. How could this happen on a deserted trail. His two remaining men were hurt but they would live to fight another day. They were down to a single crossbow and five bolts. They headed into the dense trees for more cover. The pace was less than half of what it had been. It would be many more hours in the dense brush till they found the manor house. Providing the dragons of Tyde would not return. His total control over the black two headed monster took much of his energy, the fog only added to his load, plus the using his dark sense to seek out the sheilder. The dragon attack was unforeseen. He had underestimated the small green dragons for the last time.

Chapter Eighteen

(An impasse)

Zara and her two siblings buzzed the manor house before landing in the now nearly empty field. They made their way to the manor house doors adjacent to the field. Jester and his sergeant came out to see them. Jester kneeled and picked up Zara. She trilled and pressed against him. The other two wasted no time in occupying the sergeant's broad shoulders. Jester looked bemused as the sergeant stood very still with his new found friends, looking at each in turn, then turning both his palms upwards to Jester. "Sergeant, I must say, parenthood becomes you, really." He laughed. The sergeant shot him a look, and then smiled at the two on his shoulders, unsure of what to do next. Jester let him work that part out for himself and touched Zara's head. His eyebrows went up even further than his sergeants. He was able to 'see' what Zara had witnessed during their patrol. A sense of unease grew in him now. The news of the tall man wasn't good at all. It would not be long before they were here. Jester let Zara know how well she'd done, including the other two. The dragons flapped their wings excitedly. As usual, he had to pull Zara's left wing away from his face so he could see. He sent them over to the other dragons remaining to share the story with them. The dragons would now move indoors. Into the manor hall. He wanted Tantrus up on her ceiling perch. King was just too large to accommodate so he was sent to Jester's own troops across the courtyard. His sergeant ran ahead to explain to the men why the biggest dragon in any of the known kingdoms was going to be their new mascot! The sergeant laughed to himself at the very thought of it. He would emphasize to the men about not being 'underfoot' with the gentle beast. Jester opened the large doors to the manor hall with the help of several of Dunvegan's guards. He sent a guard to get Myra and her father. Another two new little dragons were sent to his castle to confirm the safe arrival of Shandahr and Ronald. Things were about to be siege like, very quickly now. Jester made one last quick trip to the dragon stone on Dunvegan's property. He held the stone with both hands, and touched his forehead against the cool stone itself. All the dragons in Tyde now knew of the situation as of the moment. It would not be long now, till they were all called into service. As Jester left the magical stone and headed back to the manor, three shadows closed the gap from the forest to the remains of the outer stone wall surrounding Dunvegan's manor.

They waited till the man had returned into the old manor house. Vectus finally stood. His eyes glowed in the darkness. This was the source from where the other dark power emanated. He could feel his skin prickle slightly as they made their way along the far edge of the wall that surrounded the manor house. The ground still smelled of dragons. He knew he had to be very careful from here on in. Although he had encountered others with the dark powers, none had been this strong before. The three sat in the burnt grass by the old stone wall. For now, they would wait. Vectus used his powers to 'see' into the manor. What he saw startled even him. It was the interior of his cabin on the now sunken flagship. Whoever had the dark powers in the manor, had reflected his vision back to a simple recent memory of his own. He pressed his power a little further but saw only darkness. In his anger and frustration he stopped seeing and with the power, forced a stone from the wall nearest them, high into the air and over the field. The stone was head sized and arced over the field. He was sure it would just land in the trees over and past the courtyard. It didn't. By sheer fluke, it landed directly on King's snout, shattering into small pieces. The resting dragon opened both eyes at once! Jester's men had retired quietly to their tents before the stone had struck him. He let out a low growl and stood. The growl could be heard clearly for some distance. The doors to the manor opened and several people emerged. Vectus watched closely as they walked towards the courtyard. He and his remaining two men slipped closer to the open doorway. Just then, another figure stepped from the manor's doorway. In two large strides, Vectus grabbed the figure and dragged it backwards, away from the door and around the corner. His power stopped any sound from escaping the struggling person. One of his men quickly wrapped a hood over their capture. They silently left for the cover of the trees and were on the path back towards the coast. Vectus soon realized the now hooded figure wasn't the only one with the dark powers. Although they were above average, this was not the person doing the blocking or shielding the dragons of Tyde. He stopped his men holding the still struggling figure. "Remove the hood" he commanded. The hood was pulled off roughly and Vectus was face to face with the Grey Princess. She tried to speak, but his power easily kept her mute. Vectus regarded her another moment longer. "Replace the hood. Bring her." They hurried down the path towards the coast. Vectus knew she would be missed shortly. He smiled inwardly at his great good fortune. He knew they would be desperate to get her back. The Grey Princess would be a most useful tool, in the demise of this kingdom. As they neared the coast the fog was thick and visibility was no more than twenty paces. They were climbing down the rocks to the waters edge when the sounds of distant horns could be heard. Even in the thick fog, signal fires were being lit all down the shoreline. Vectus placed his hand on the Grey Princess's head, she went limp and was dropped on the wooden planks of the longboat. His two remaining men pulled hard on the oars. As they left the shoreline the fog began to thin out. His fleet was just ahead. The black hulls were barely visible on the moonless sea. As they boarded one of the ships, Vectus could hear dragon wings knifing through the air high overhead. He pulled the hood off his prisoner. She lay on the deck, eyes open, unable to speak or move. She saw the dragons circle high overhead, the stars were their backdrop. Vectus looked down at the Grey Princess and grabbed her firmly by one wrist and pulled her savagely upwards to her feet. His grip on her wrist was like a steel vice. He removed all her rings from her fingers, dislocating several fingers in the process. When he finished removing the rings, two of his men dragged her below decks and chained her up to a sail locker hatch. Her feet barely touched the floor. The heavy door was closed and locked behind them. Vectus took the rings and placed them in a leather wrap, and tied it tightly in a small bundle. The little dragons still circled high above the ships. He waved an archer over to him. The bundle was placed on a long bolt and tied tightly to it. He pointed upwards and waited. The archer pulled hard on the bow's

drawstring and shot the bolt straight up into the circling
dragons. The bolt narrowly missed impaling two of them
as it rocketed past them, upwards towards the night sky.
Because of the imbalance caused by the package tied to
the bolt, it gyrated in an odd way. Its speed diminished as
the gyrating grew in its intensity. The dragons heard the
strange sound and were curious. One gave chase, realizing
something was attached to the bolt itself. The little green
dragon caught up to the bolt easily and grabbed it with his
rear legs. He spiralled down to the others and all but one
returned to the manor at speed. One stayed behind to
keep watch over the ship with the Grey Princess onboard.
The others raced over the treetops at speed, feeling as one
with the skies. As they approached the curiously burnt
circle on the rocky hilltop, they slowed and began a rapid
descent into the courtyard of the manor. There were many
men waiting for them, Jester stood in front with Zara on
his shoulder. The dragons landed together and parted for
the one with the bolt. He dropped it at Jester's feet,
flapping his wings excitedly. "What have we here my little
friend?" he said, bending over to pick up the bolt. He
stood and untied the bundle. He looked down at Myra's
rings in his hand. He knew everyone of them well. Sir
Dunvegan looked at Jester. "We must do something, we
must…" His voice caught in his throat. He just stared
down at the timeworn cobble stones where they stood, at a
loss for words. Jester knelt and placed his hand on the

little dragon's head that had caught the bolt. "She is alive, on one of his ships." He stood and looked at his sergeant. "Vectus now has bargaining power. Except he doesn't bargain. He just takes. I'd send the dragons and men now to burn him to ash and end this now! Myra is on one of those ships out there, alive for the present. This changes everything, and nothing." he said flatly. His sergeant cleared his throat. "He now has a shield of sorts, to use against you, and the dragons. This is something we couldn't have planned for, let alone imagined." "If I may interrupt?" asked Dunvegan. "No one expected my daughter to be kidnapped. Vectus was looking for me I'm afraid. He can sense my powers with the darker magic, and was able to track our whereabouts using his ability as a seer. Myra was in the wrong place at the wrong time. He knows he has someone special, perhaps not exactly what he was after, but useful nonetheless. The next move still belongs to Vectus at this point. He must know there is a dragon master now, but not who. I have been using my powers to shield the dragons and even you Jester, from his 'vision'. As far as I can tell, he is still blind to our capabilities at this point. I have no doubt in my mind he will wish to trade my daughter for me. On my death, he will have a clear view of all our preparations and abilities. Those he can use against us in a big way. He has no honour about him, there would be no guarantee Myra would even be returned, or alive, either way. We are at an impasse I'm afraid. He won't waste much time making his demands known, of that, I'm sure." They all began to head into the manor hall again when the little dragons startled and hissed out loud. A large dragon streaked overhead in the predawn light. It was black and had chains dangling from its legs. Jester could feel Zara tense on his shoulder. The dragon made a steep turn to the right, spilling air in readiness for a landing. Everyone in the courtyard scattered to make room as the down blast of air hit the ground. The black two headed dragon settled onto the cobblestones in the courtyard. Even King had gotten to his feet now. All of them were on edge. Astride the great black dragon was Vectus himself. The dragon's heads were in constant motion, looking every which way, as if it would be attacked at any moment. It was truly unsettled, fighting the dark magic that held it in control from Vectus. The tall man dismounted from the dragon. He carried a heavy coarse blanket with something rolled up inside it. He walked halfway to where Jester and Dunvegan stood. He removed his helmet, revealing very close cropped hair and three parallel scars that ran from behind his head, diagonally across his face to the corner of his mouth. The old wound had been from a young dragon trying to escape his hold on it. He had destroyed the poor creature immediately by strangulation. His face was set in a scowl of disdain. Neither Jester nor Dunvegan could ever imagine a smile on that face. Vectus regarded the group of men. He was unimpressed. He spoke in English, clearly, despite an accent. "As you're aware by now, I have the Grey Princess as my prisoner. I'll trade you her life for yours!" He nodded towards Sir Dunvegan. "I will consider sparing the rest of your sad lives with an unconditional surrender of the kingdom. You have until midday to make your decision." He turned and walked a few paces towards the black dragon, then turned again. "These are pathetic scouts" he stated as he let the blanket unravel. The very dead body of the missing scout dragon rolled onto the stones. It's neck broken. He looked directly at Jester. "If I see one of these near my fleet, the trade is off. The woman dies." He turned his back on the group and mounted the dragon. It shot skyward, uneven lengths of blackened, iron chain, trailed out below it. The down draught from its wings blew the lifeless body off to the side of the courtyard. Zara trilled quietly and ran to the dead dragon. She rested her muzzle on its head and closed her eyes. In a few moments, the other little dragons joined her and did the same. Jester placed his hand on Dunvegan's shoulder and looked down. "My friend, as my sergeant so eloquently put it, the anvil has just dropped. We need to rescue Myra quickly. Vectus has the upper hand now, and I won't have him with any advantages if I can help it!" "Jester, what possibly can we do for her right now? I must turn myself over to him immediately, or we all will suffer the consequences of our inaction." said Dunvegan. "Sir, I

have to disagree with you. There is no guarantee Vectus
will release Myra even if you turn yourself in to him. I for
one don't trust him in any way. We are more than ready
compared to the last invasion. Myra's capture wasn't
foreseen. It's an added complication we need to deal with,
the sooner the better I say! I have an Idea." Jester and Sir
Dunvegan slowly walked back into the manor's great hall.
Dunvegan was resigned to the fact that he must trade
places with his daughter. Jester sat him at the table in the
hall, Tantrus was back on the floor with a decidedly angry
dragon look to her eyes. Jester knelt in front of her and
placed his hand on her muzzle. He thought the words, 'do
you want to be in on her rescue? I have a plan that has a
chance it might work'…he stayed that way for what
seemed like an eternity. Tantrus snorted her consent to
Jester's plan. He opened the great doors to the manor hall
and she made a hasty exit into the dawn's growing light.
"Sir Dunvegan, bear with me till midday. If this idea of
mine goes according to plan, Myra will be home for the
midday meal!" Dunvegan's eyebrows rose and he seemed
to protest, but thought better of it and his shoulders sank
back down again. "Promise me you'll stay put till midday.
The kingdom cannot afford to loose you at this point in
time. Use your powers to let Myra know we are coming
for her very soon. Get her to create some rain, thunder
and lightening. I need rougher waters and many
distractions for Vectus's fleet." Jester grabbed Dunvegan's

face in both of his hands and made eye contact with him. Almost nose to nose. That got his attention. "I mean now sir!" He turned and left the hall. His sergeant was just outside the huge doors. "Sergeant! We are going to mount as rescue for Myra. Have the men ready as quickly as possible!" He stopped and stared. All his men were mounted and ready to ride. Tantrus, along with all the little green dragons, including Zara were assembled in the courtyard. "What took you so long sergeant? You're slipping my friend!" Both men laughed and walked to the assembled men and dragons. "Men, we have a rescue to perform in classic rescue style. Here is the plan, such as it is. We will head to the coast. You will assist with the setting up of any final preparations for the invasion. The dragons and I are going to swim out to the fleet, undercover of a storm that will soon be upon them. Rescue the Grey Princess, and I will swim with her to shore with Zara. The other dragons will begin an organized burn of every ship Vectus has on the water. Your job is to train the long bows on the black two headed beast under Vectus's control. Kill it if you can. The rest of the kingdoms dragons fly to the coast as soon as I'm back on dry land with the Princess. Am I clear on this?" The men cheered. "Then off with you now! Godspeed, and be safe if you can." The sergeant cleared his throat. "Sir, your horse is ready, will you lead?" Jester placed both hands on his sergeant's shoulders. "You will lead them. Tantrus has offered me a ride to the shoreline. We'll land south of the fleet, just out of eyesight to them, and then swim for it. Not to worry, I'll cover myself in cooking fat for water resistance, and yes, dragons swim as well as they fly! I just hope Myra can summon a suitable storm for our cover!" The sergeant stood at attention and saluted his friend. "Godspeed to you my friend. Be successful!" The sergeant mounted his horse and the men were off at full gallop. Jester waved to Dunvegan, who had appeared in the library window. In ten strides he was at Tantrus's side and climbed onto her back. Zara scrambled up and was in her place just in front of him, like when on his horse. Tantrus stood and with several wing beats, they rose into the sunrise and headed towards the coast.

The feeling of flying was a little scary. Jester knew he had to rescue Myra or Vectus would gain the upper hand which he would not allow to happen this time. His natural fear of heights was displaced by the sheer beauty of flying, and the imminent rescue attempt. The little green dragons trailed out behind Tantrus, keeping a fairly loose formation. The treetops hurtled past just below them. It was like a green blur beneath them. In a few moments they would be landing on the southern coast. Jester breathed deeply, it was times like this he was truly alive and at one with the dragons. Tantrus shot a small fireball upwards in agreeance. All the little dragons did the same.

A dark shadow fell over Jester and Tantrus. He looked up as King crossed over them and joined the formation. Jester marvelled at the sheer size of King. For all his mass and weight, he was most graceful in the air. He noticed the sky was clouding over at the coast. Myra had gotten the message! A brief flash of lightening arced in the distance. Good, it would be all he needed. Tantrus had guided them well south of the fleet. Jester could see the ocean now. The first drops of rain began to fall.

They landed as a single grouping along a wide deserted beach. Jester slid from Tantrus's back onto the soft sand, Zara on his shoulder as usual. The dragons created a large circle around him. He held out his arms and knelt in the sand. Today will be a test of your abilities as dragons. We are all in grave danger now. Some of us will not return if things go badly from here. This rescue will require all of us to swim only. Unless we are discovered, everything will be accomplished in or under the water. No one will fly until we are at this beach again for the journey home. If Vectus sees us or any of his men, the rescue will have failed. The Grey princess will die at his hands. All of you here know this evil man and what he will do. Our little scout was only the first to die. I will only ask you to follow me in this rescue. I do not command it. If you wish to wait here, I will understand. The plan is simple enough. We will swim to the fleet from

Ionicus, locate the Grey Princess, free her, then burn the
fleet where it sits and return home. I won't know till we
are amongst the ships, where she is. Let me be clear on
this, we cannot be spotted or it's all over for her. I know
you all can swim very well indeed, we need to be out of
sight, out of mind. The exact ship, we will deal with as
needed, to get her out and to the shore safely. Vectus will
do all he can to prevent it. Make no mistakes in this. If he
catches one of you, it will be your death. It's that simple.
Watch for the black two headed dragon. It is under
Vectus's direct control. If it comes to a choice, burn it.
Burn it completely. It will be a salvation for it I'm sure. Its
time to begin this. Jester stood and removed all his light
armour, but kept his sword with him. He waded into the
sea. All of the dragons followed. Tantrus paused to let
him swim out to her with Zara. He held on to her folded
wing and they all began the swim out to the Ionicus fleet.
The dragons swam with ease. Although the sky was their
element, they were very proficient swimmers and seemed
at home in the salty water. A few of the little ones gagged
occasionally on the salt water, but soon learned to keep
their mouths shut tightly. The rain began to fall heavily
now. Jester new she was still safe, for now. After a while,
he could make out the dark hulls and masts of the ships.
Their sails hung lifeless from the stays. As they got closer,
he could see only a single lookout in the crow's nest of
each ship. The little dragons were nearly invisible in the

water, just an occasional snout for a brief instant. Dragons needed little air when swimming, so they were able to stay clear of the surface for long periods. Tantrus could stay underwater for a very long time, but kept the intervals short for Jester's sake. As they neared the fleet, they swung around to approach from the rear of the ships. The least visibility was rearward for the soldiers onboard. It was a real downpour now. Any trace of the dragon's movements in the water was gone due to the heavy rain. The water ran freely from the decks and railings above. The footing would be very slippery as well.

They had slowly joined in with the fleet now and moved gently from ship to ship. Jester would know when they reached the ship with Myra and Vectus aboard. After passing a dozen more blackened hulls, Jester could feel Tantrus tense up suddenly. She stopped swimming and drifted with the ships. He knew they were close now. Even Zara seemed fidgety now. As they rounded the stern of the nearest ship, Jesters breath stopped momentarily. The ship ahead of them had a banner with a crest depicting a sword rammed through a dragon skull. Along side was a longboat, with a solitary guard sitting in the middle of it. The rain ran off his battle armour as he sat motionless, awaiting his watch replacement. The new guard climbed awkwardly down the rope netting laid over the side of the ship. The two men said a few words and the other man climbed upwards to the railings and disappeared across the deck. The replacement sat where the other had, now on duty and miserable with the rain. Jester touched Tantrus's head briefly, then pushed away from her and swam underwater to the stern of the longboat. He grabbed the rudder with both hands and pulled it as hard as he could off to the side. The rudder's handle struck the sitting guard hard across his left forearm. Startled, the guard rose and stepped to the rear of the longboat. He bent over the transom to see what was happening with the rudder. It was his final mistake in life. Tantrus, with jaws wide open, simply took the guard head first, quietly over the side; His last screams were deep under the fleet as the dragon's jaws crushed him easily. She spat him out and his remains with the heavy, now flattened battle armour took him straight downwards. Jester pulled himself into the longboat, then Zara and six other little dragons. As they were about to climb the rope netting to the decks above, King came upwards directly below the ships hull and began to almost imperceptively tow it away from the other ships nearby. Tantrus had now bitten off the bottom of Vectus's ships rudder. The rain was coming down in torrents. Any sound of splintering wood was lost to the storm. Jester peered over the edge of the ships hull, no one was on deck for the moment. He sent a dragon to the crows nest to deal with the lookout.

The lookout had been in the crows nest for many hours. He was wet, cold and stiff from not moving. He suddenly felt an increase in weight on his helmet. He reached upwards and felt something cold. He flipped his visor up for a better look and was met with a set of needle like teeth and jaws across his face. As he inhaled to shout out, his lungs were filled with dragon flame. He crumpled to the side of the crows nest. A thin trail of smoke dissipated from his nose. Jester carefully entered the companionway downwards to the front quarters of the ship. He had a choice of three doors ahead. Zara ran to the center door and looked at him. Jester pushed slowly and the door opened a crack. The cabin was full of anchor chain and ropes. The base of the forward mast was centered in the small cabin. Myra was firmly tied to a sail locker. Two guards sat facing him, both lulled to a doze by the quietness. Zara darted in as well as several other dragons. Jester eased the door open further. Zara and another leapt onto the guards chests, knocking them onto their backs. The dragon flame down the windpipe prevented any sound escaping the two. Jester cut the ropes binding Myra to the locker and she swooned. She was either drugged or Vectus had some control over her. He picked her up and headed to the companionway. As he reached the railing with the rope netting he saw it had been cut free and was lying in a heap in the longboat fifteen feet below. His mind raced. Who had done this…he froze for a moment, and turned. Vectus stood across the deck from him with crossed arms. "So, I see you have taken matters into your own hands, 'Dragon Master of Tyde.' A very stupid and predictable move I might add. Somehow I expected more of you. A typically disappointing move." Zara ran to Jester's feet and hissed loudly at Vectus. "Is this where I'm supposed to panic and throw myself off the ship?" Jester made a small move with his hand to get Zara to stand behind him. She reluctantly did so. The upper hand was still not entirely in Vectus's hands. Jester made a fake step backwards, and 'tripped' over Zara. With all his strength he lifted Myra up and over his head from his 'trip' and dropped her overboard. He turned in mock surprise as she hit the water. Tantrus took her away swiftly. Vectus ran to the railing and looked down only to see foam on the rain swept waters. Jester was ready for this and grabbed Vectus behind his head and slammed it into the railing with as much force as he could muster. He heard the man's nose break on the stout wooden hand rail. He then grabbed Vectus by the shoulders and pushed his upper body down hard and raised his right knee into his upper chest with everything he had. He pulled out his sword and was about to finish Vectus once and for all when the ship suddenly pitched sideways. King was pushing the ship nearly out of the water. Jester slid across the deck to the other side and jumped into the churning sea. As Vectus staggered from the blows, the remaining dragons set fire to his ship with the hottest flame they could muster, and then leapt into the storm tossed sea. All of them swam hard towards the shore. Jester held Zara and another dragon by their bodies and let them pull him from the zig zag of dark hulls towards the shoreline. Several of the Ionicus archers shot bolts from their cross bows at the departing dragons. All of the bolts struck and killed a dozen men on the adjacent ship as the new flagship abruptly veered sideways. Everyone grabbed onto a railing as the entire ship was turned over in the churning waters. King forced the ship under the surface and it split in two from his downwards push. His massive tail whipped downwards from the effort, cutting three more ships in half. He let his weight sink him momentarily, and then headed away towards shore. His massive wake caused several more ships to ram into one another. Masts snapped and wood splinters flew every where. Twenty of the little dragons burst from the waters and returned to burn many more of the Ionicus ships before turning for the shoreline. It was chaos for the enemy fleet. Not a ship left could steer. All the rudders had been eaten through and the ropes bitten clean off, that would launch the longboats. Any ship not on fire by now was severely damaged and no longer seaworthy. Vectus was barely able to breath and couldn't see much from the well placed blows from the Dragon Master of

Tyde. His blood ran freely from his shattered nose onto his rain soaked tunic and shiny wet armour, as he clung to the burning and slowly sinking stern of his ship. So now it begins.

Chapter Nineteen

(The dragons unleashed)

Sir Dunvegan sat at his desk in the library. The rain pelted the window creating a rippled view of the outside. He was worried for his daughter and the fate of Jester, the dragon master. It had been a loosely planned rescue. It had a partial chance of success, but there was no alternative, no time, and no powers of persuasion would have any effect on Vectus. Jester was a good man at heart. Clever, brave beyond anyone he'd ever met. Yet, impulsive, and brash. He smiled a little at that. The perfect man for the job he thought. No one would be able to second guess his plans. Jester was a deviation from a more practical military thinking person. A creative general, who was not afraid to take risks. It was himself who took the greatest risks, not his men or the dragons in this case. His thoughts were interrupted suddenly by men shouting in the courtyard. Dunvegan stood to look out the window. Tantrus, along with several dozen of the Zara dragons landed in the field beside the courtyard. He ran to the main entrance. Tantrus had Myra in her jaws, carefully protected from her sharp teeth with a great wad of seaweed that had been ripped from the sea floor. She held her mouth open wide so his men could pick her up and bring her to the manor. Dunvegan stepped out into the rain. "Take her to the library at once! In front of the fire place." He followed the men into the library. With a quick movement of his hand, a large warming fire ignited in the grate. Myra was very wet, cold, and smelled strongly of fish. "Lay her by the fire. We need to warm her quickly." Dunvegan pulled some seaweed from her and knelt beside her. "Thank you, anything more and I'll let you know." said Dunvegan. The men left the manor and stood in the courtyard. The sergeant-at-arms spoke. "Listen up, so far we have no word on Jester. I say we ride for the coast. He may need our assistance, half will remain here as a guard," The troop mounted their horses and left at a gallop. The trail was sodden, but the tree canopy kept the rain from hitting them directly while they made their way to the coast. The men noticed a half dozen or so of the little green dragons had joined them. They eased past them, and flew just in front.

Jester's sergeant stood at the beach with the many archers gathered and ready. The first group of dragons were returning from the now burning fleet. He hoped none of them would use him as a perch. He laughed at that. He was actually beginning to feel more comfortable around them. He'd had a cat when he was very young, although he seemed to remember it was actually the cat that had him. He did admire the dragons for their assistance in this new invasion. It was they who defeated the last one, he hoped it would be that way once again. This Vectus was as close to pure evil as he'd ever known anyone to be. His death would be a good cause in his books! The greasy black smoke roiled from the burning ships. More of the little dragons exited the water and ran up the beach. The sergeant was glad he wasn't on board any of those ships. As far as he could tell, none would ever make landfall, either here or Ionicus. Yet something within him said it was not the end of Vectus yet. They had only scored the first victory. The water seemed to swell upwards, as King finally surfaced. He exited the water and turned to look at the burning, sinking fleet.

A few shouts rang out along the beach. Jester, with Zara and others walked along the shore to the sergeant. "Hahah! I love it when one of your plans works out so well!" laughed the sergeant. Jester crossed both his eyes then sat in the sand. "I almost had him at sword point sergeant. I was so close to ending it all, but the ship was being destroyed from under my very feet. I was forced to make a hasty exit. I have the feeling we are not quite done with Vectus and his plans for Tyde." The sergeant sat down next to Jester. "Yes you're quite right, I can't help but feel the same way. Although I'm not sure what he can do with out his fleet now." said the sergeant.

The rain had begun to let up. The near horizon still had a pall of heavy black smoke spread across it. The invasion fleet was a shambles. Five ships remained on the surface but all were badly damaged. Their masts were at odd angles across decks, the rigging shredded and hanging down the sides of the hulls. None of the remaining ships would stay afloat much longer. Jester finally stood, still looking at the sad remains of the invasion fleet. He looked at several of the small dragons. They turned their heads towards him as if listening. Jester nodded towards the ships. They shot skywards and headed out to the five remaining ships. The sergeant got up and stood beside him. In another moment the dozen or so little dragons circled the ships. As if on cue, all of them shot the hottest flame they could muster at the ships. The inferno was nearly white hot. The dragons added more flame to the pyre. In a few moments the remaining ships slipped below the surface. They would continue to burn underwater until all the wood had been consumed. Nothing would remain. Even the iron and bronze fittings would melt and scatter on the sea floor. As the little ones returned to the shore, the sun finally came out. Jester turned to his sergeant and said, "I like this view much better, don't you?" Both men laughed and prepared to return to the manor.

The troop from Dunvegan manor arrived as the last piece of the fleet slipped below the waves. They were about to exchange greetings when the arriving troops horses reared up in panic. They all faced the sea. The water was churning white with foam and spray, where the fleet had been sunk. It was as if tens of thousands of large fish were feeding near the surface. Everyone stared in wonder at the huge commotion in the water. The sergeant turned to Jester, "This battle isn't over yet sir!" Jester yelled out, "Archers! Ready yourselves!" The archers manned the bows and swords were drawn. The churned water began to spread outwards. Jester along with all the men squinted at the raging water. Something was below the surface and rising. Dark shapes could be made out moving just below the surface, no one had seen such a thing before. Several of the rider's horses bolted towards the forest trail, dumping their riders in the process. The many dragons crowded in front of jester and his sergeant. All eyes were on the sea now. Jester noticed a lone dragon very high above them. It was one of the 'all wing' breed. It circled lazily over the churning sea water. He reached up and touched Zara briefly. She leapt skyward and with her amazing speed, rocketed upwards, nearly vertical and intercepted the huge winged dragon far above. In a moment, a dark speck began to drop from the sky. Zara had her wings tightly folded against her and she dropped back towards the beach. Her own body created a white contrail behind her, as she plummeted earthward. In true Zara fashion, she waited till the last possible moment to pull out of the dive and streaked across the beach. She pulled up hard and rolled over to be level with the beach. In a wild flapping of wings to slow herself, she landed heavily at Jester's feet. He bent and picked her up. She felt very cold to his touch from the high speed climb and dive. Jester now understood this strange commotion in the water was also happening in several other locations in the kingdom. The men everywhere were at the ready, but no one was prepared for what came next. The water seemed to explode all at once. Columns of water rose high above the choppy surface. Hundreds of them it seemed. From the columns, came the black two headed dragons. They broke away from the water and turned towards the beach. There were far too many to count. Jester could make out Vectus, riding the creature with the chains trailing from its legs. The attack had begun.

The archers shot a volley of large bolts into the air. As Vectus had planned, most bolts never made it to their target. Many of the heavy longbows failed completely!

The men were only able to use the regular longbows, with
no effect on the attacking dragons. One of the heavy
longbows had been brought out as a replacement, and
with new bolts. The archers aimed carefully and hit the
target. One of many black dragons fell to the sea. The long
heavy bolt had gone through its upper torso. The men
cheered and reloaded. All the men on the beach went to
find any further replacement bows and bolts. They kept
a sharp eye on the incoming dragons. The men on the
beach at least were equipped with dragon scale shields
which would offer protection from a blast of dragon fire.
Jester sent the other men into the forest edge to look for
shields and more heavy longbows with bolts. He quickly
dispersed the little dragons onto the tree tops. There, they
could try and burn any dragons flying over the tree line
along the beach. The large dragons had already taken to
the air and were attacking from behind. The big dragons
could not burn another dragon like the little ones could.
They relied on flying ability, sharp teeth and claws. A large
bite out of a wing would end the flight in a crash. These
crashes happened rarely, as dragons seldom fight each
other, but are almost always fatal to the dragon. Jester
knew this of course. Vectus had taken the free will of
those now attacking and turned the tables on nature itself.
As far as Jester was concerned, Vectus was the prime target
in this battle. He must be defeated at any cost. "Sergeant,
I'm heading back to the manor. I need Dunvegan now.

Try your best to hold on here. Take out as many dragons as possible!" He ran over to Tantrus and was away in moments.

Jester and Tantrus raced over the trees faster than he ever thought possible. A green flash passed them, and then slowed. It was Zara. She flew close enough to touch. Jester didn't dare take a hand off Tantrus at that speed. The wind would surely pull him off! They arrived at the manor's courtyard. Jester slid off Tantrus's shoulders and ran for the manor. Zara scampered close behind, and then leapt up on his shoulder. He entered the library and found Dunvegan and Myra sitting at the fireplace. He hugged her tightly. Sir Dunvegan stood, "Jester, careful now, she is a little better now, but still shaking the effects of Vectus's control. She will recover fully I'm sure. What is happening at the coast?" Jester sat beside Myra and explained the situation. Dunvegan paced the room while he listened. "In short, Sir, we are in for a battle with the dragons." Dunvegan went to his desk and rummaged through the drawings till he found the black, two headed dragon. "These are almost as rare as your Zara. To have arrived with as many as you say is truly amazing. Both heads are separate with the necks joining at the torso. They share all other features of a normal dragon body. They are, however not twice as smart with two heads. The brain is split, or shared between the heads. Their only advantage is their eyesight from what I understand. One can look up, the other down, or even rearwards. Almost impossible to attack with out it seeing what's coming. A definite advantage in this attack." Jester cleared his throat. "Is there any drawbacks to having two heads and one shared brain? I'm looking for anything I can use against them. However trivial it may seem." Dunvegan regarded the drawing again. Myra whispered something. Jester leaned in towards her. "Myra, say that again for me. Please." Myra whispered again. "Use three, three..." Her voice trailed off. "Three? Use three?" said Jester. He looked at Dunvegan with his palms up. "Three, Use three." Repeated Dunvegan, slowly, as if memorizing words he'd never heard before. Myra was unable to add any further to the question. She looked tired and in need of rest. Dunvegan's shoulders slumped. "I'm sorry Jester, I can't think of what she means at this moment." Jester held Myra another moment, then got up. "Sir, I must get back to the men now. Send a messenger, dragon or man, if you manage to decipher what she said." Dunvegan raised a hand in farewell, and Jester, with Zara back on his shoulders, left the manor. Tantrus was ready for the swift flight back to the coast. As Jester and Zara passed a row of banners on several waiting horses, he saw the crest that was depicted on his sword. He stopped suddenly, causing Zara to somersault to the ground. Two dragons and one hand. Three. His skin prickled. He ran to Tantrus

and placed his hand on her head, then after a moment
dashed back inside the manor. Zara sat and watched as
he ran to Tantrus then back inside the manor. Her head
turning to follow him. After a moment, she went back
into the manor in time to see Dunvegan heading to
the main hall. Jester was right behind with Myra in his
arms. She followed them to a table and chairs set near
the huge 'dragon doors' at the rear of the hall. Dunvegan
made a small movement with both his hands and the
great doors slid open. Tantrus was waiting and as the
doorway became wide enough, entered the hall with her
head lowered beside Myra. Jester placed Myra's hand on
Tantrus's head and held it there with his own. He closed
his eyes and lowered his head in concentration. He waved
to Zara to get on the table and placed his other hand on
her head. The familiar coolness ran through him from
Tantrus to Zara. He could feel Myra as well, but distant.
Her thoughts were jumbled and muddied, but some were
clear enough. Jester asked quietly to tell him more about
the three. Three what? He waited. Both dragons did what
they could to help Myra clear the cobwebs left by Vectus.
Three, three, oh yes of course, three. Try three, not one,
not two,…three! Three will do it very nicely I think. Jester
was not following this thread very well. Three dragons.
Two dragons, one brave knight. Two knights and one
dragon. Jester's eyes went big suddenly. Even Tantrus and
Zara reacted to that. Jester released his hands from the

dragons and Myra. "Yes, it's clear. Why didn't I think of this?' Jester looked at Dunvegan and smacked his right palm into his forehead. "So simple, so simple!" he said. He briefly touched the two dragons in turn. They were off to the coast once again. Jester carried Myra back to the library and placed her in a chair by the warming fire. He kissed the top of her head and hugged a puzzled Dunvegan. "Ask your daughter when she recovers a little more! I have a battle to win and a score to settle!"

Prior to leaving the manor, Jester made another visit to the dragon stone. He placed one hand on either side, and then leaned into it until his forehead touched the cool stone. He wondered how many other dragon masters had done this before him. It was a humbling experience and he'd hoped that he would prove himself worthy. Jester closed his eyes, and let the coolness of the ancient stone flow into him. It was a lot like the feeling he had when touching Tantrus and Zara. He asked the dragons of Tyde to meet at the big clearing by his castle. A new plan was in the works, one that he hoped would end the attack by Vectus, and put and end to him and any ideas of returning. He slowly released his hold on the stone. A warmth radiated from the previously cool surface. As he turned to leave, Zara trilled at him. She had her copper chain mail armour in her mouth. Jester knelt and fastened it to her. He stood and waited for Tantrus to lower herself to the ground.

He climbed onto her back and they rose skyward, headed for the clearing he first 'met' this amazing creature, Myra and Zara. His life was never the same after that fateful day, and he would not have changed it even if he could. His thoughts faded quickly as Tantrus began to slow and banked gently to the left. Her wings began to rise higher as she spilled air from under them. The ground came up fast and then they were down in the grasses. Dragons from all over the kingdom began arriving in the clearing. In a very short time it was near full. The dragons who could not find room enough to land simply circled overhead, creating a living vortex of dragons. Jester made his way to the center of the clearing and raised both hands skyward. The dragons made several circles, surrounding him, each dragon was able to touch the next. Zara was on his right shoulder. He knelt in the grass and placed his right hand on her head. He was now connected to all the dragons there. His plan was quite simple, but required timing in its execution. Jester lowered his head and closed his eyes. 'We are about to begin a battle to save our kingdom and way of life. Both human and dragons. We ask for simple freedom, nothing more. Vectus brings nothing but evil submission to his will in everything. If he is successful, we will all be slaves to his every whim. Tyde will no longer exist and will become what Ionicus is now, a terrible wasteland of evil and greed. Free will, no longer having a place. We are going to face an enemy that will be relentless. A two headed dragon sees in many directions at once, but not three at a time. We will attack each dragon in three's. Two to occupy the heads, one to kill from behind, above, or below. The little ones have a flame that will take them down. Beware of your wings, if bitten or torn, you can't fly. I'll stay with Tantrus, but any large dragon can carry a knight. We will begin immediately. Godspeed to all of you! Jester took a deep breath and stood. He raised both hands skyward and the dragons began to head for the coast.

Tantrus rose on her hind legs, and with a powerful down stroke of her great wings, she and Jester left the ground and began the first wave of the attack on the dragons from Ionicus. Jester drew his beautiful sword and held it high. The sunlight gleamed from the rare metal and he felt empowered to take on Vectus once and for all. Instead of flying low to the tree tops, they climbed high above the kingdom of Tyde. In the distance, the battle for the coast had begun. Smoke could be seen coming from the shore. The black two headed dragons swooped down on the men at the huge longbows. Their flame shot downwards and the men raised the dragon scale shields. Many of the bows were burnt by the dragon fire, but were replaced quickly with new ones. The giant long bows had dropped and killed a number of the enemy dragons. The bodies clearly visible on the beach and in the water. As they neared the beach, Zara and another dragon joined Jester and Tantrus and they began the first attack run. Jester targeted a two headed dragon right next to Vectus… Tantrus swooped over the dragon and grabbed the right head in her powerful rear claws and pulled hard. A little dragon drew the attention of the second head by flying just close enough to allow it the false possibility of catching it in its jaws. Zara came up from below every ones line of sight and blasted the poor creature with her hottest flame, from the base of its two necks, clear to its tail, the deep blue flame did what it did best. The dragon erupted in flames and dropped from the sky! Vectus banked his dragon hard to the left and climbed higher. Several more of his dragons burst into flames and fell to the sea. The dragon master of Tyde must die and quickly. Vectus continued his steep turning climb looking for the dragon master. Jester and the dragons were taking down the two headed creatures with great success. Elsewhere the story was the same. Vectus was at the extremes of his power over the numbers of dragons he could control at once. He found himself unable to release the dead and dying from his power. He felt a weakness he had never felt before, as he hunted for Jester. Then off near the tree line, he finally spotted him. He forced his own dragon into a near vertical dive towards Jester. The dragon master of Tyde was lining up another attack run when suddenly the sun disappeared and Tantrus was violently pulled nearly sideways. The two headed dragon had both sets of jaws and teeth clamped down on her tail, and was pulling her further off to the right. Jester clung to her neck tightly to keep his balance. They were now moving backwards through the air. Tantrus was unable to control her flight. Her tail was being pulled and bitten viciously as the two headed creature used its weight and momentum from the high speed dive to pull her downwards. Jester pulled his sword from the scabbard and took a swing at the creature trying to kill Tantrus. It was too far from him to reach with the sword. Zara broke right and was about to hit Vectus with a blast of blue flame, when another black dragon shoved her with its tail, sending her spiralling downwards and away from Vectus. The second little dragon passed close to Vectus and he unexpectedly reached out with lightening speed and grabbed it from the air, snapping its neck. In a single heartbeat it fell from the sky. Its lifeless body fell into the treetops and disappeared. Tantrus was out of control, her great wings strained to pull her forwards to no avail. The canopy of trees was coming up fast. The little dragons could not use their hottest flame to destroy the beast Vectus rode for fear of killing Tantrus. At the last second, the two headed dragon let go of Tantrus, its leg chains crashing over top of the trees churning loose leaves and branches before gaining height. Tantrus and Jester were not so lucky. They smashed hard into the forest canopy and disappeared from view. Heavy branches and several tree trunks exploded into splinters. Jester was thrown from Tantrus. He crashed and bounced like a doll through the trees and landed hard on the forest floor. It was all he could do to just breathe in short gasping breaths. Tantrus snapped and crushed several large trees till she hit heavily on the ground near Jester. One wing badly damaged from the jagged, splintered remains of the trees. Her tail broken by the impact, she laid on her side unable to move. She was dimly aware of the little dragons rocketing past over head.

Zara had witnessed the terrible crash and shot downwards into the trees herself. She landed near Tantrus and trilled at her. Tantrus had her eyes closed now and breathed steadily but in short shallow breaths. Zara knew she was badly hurt and managed to touch her right front leg. She let her know she would be guarded and watched. Several other little dragons landed nearby and stayed with her. Zara scurried over to Jester and trilled loudly at him. She pushed under his arm and leaned against him. He moved slightly and struggled to place a hand on her head. Other than perhaps a broken rib, he had been winded by the fall and would recover. Several more little dragons landed and came to Zara. They touched wings briefly and would remain on guard with Jester, and then Zara shot skyward. She blasted out of the canopy and spotted Vectus not far off. She knew he must be destroyed somehow. Many of the black, two headed dragons had been killed but there were many more. Some were still coming from the sea. She veered to the left and headed for the manor house at high speed, just above the trees.

Dunvegan sat at his library desk staring at the drawings of dragons. Myra sat next to him, still not feeling herself. She looked at her father. "There is something we are missing. Something that could help us in this battle, I can feel it. I just can't see it yet, but its there." Sir Dunvegan turned and looked at her. He was about to speak when Zara landed on the thick stone window sill and entered the library. Myra stood. "Zara!" Zara jumped onto the desk top and trilled at her. She looked at Dunvegan, Myra reached out and rubbed her jaw. Zara could feel by her touch that she was still suffering from the effects of whatever Vectus had done to her aboard the ship. Her fingers were cold and ring less. Zara's eyes widened and she scurried across the desk, knocking drawings onto the floor. "What on earth has gotten into her?" said Dunvegan. Zara looked about the room and saw what she was looking for. At the far end of the fireplace, on the great mantle piece, were Myra's rings. Zara flew across the room and landed on the mantle, knocking more of Dunvegan's treasures to the floor. She spotted the ring with the special crest on it and gently picked it up with her mouth, then flew back to the desk and dropped it in front of Myra. She trilled loudly and bumped her hand with her muzzle. "Thank you Zara, I'd forgotten about them in my current state." She looked at her father and then placed the ring on her right index finger. It was as if she had been doused by a pail of ice water! Myra held her hand away from her and looked at her father in disbelief. "Zara! How did you know?" Zara trilled again and she picked her up in her arms. "It worked! The ring, I'm feeling it more than ever. I'm truly myself again." She held Zara close for a moment. Jester and Tantrus are in great danger! I must get to them quickly. She put Zara back down on the desk and went to the window. The dragon that had suffered the broken wing a few days ago was out side. She knew it would take her to them. Without hesitation she climbed out the window and ran to the waiting dragon. Zara trilled again at Dunvegan and launched herself off the desk and out the window. With a great down rush of air, they cleared the tree tops and headed to where Jester and Tantrus lay.

Jester was dimly aware of the little dragon's presence. He thought he could hear horses and men's voices coming closer to where he laid. He tried to move, but a stabbing pain in his side prevented him from further

movement. He recognised his sergeant's voice as they
came nearer. "Over here! Quickly now!" said the sergeant.
He knelt down beside his friend. "Jester, what have you
done to yourself man. We saw the crash and came right
away. Can you move at all?" asked the sergeant. Jester
was only able to breathe and nod his head. The sergeant
looked round and saw Tantrus a dozen or so paces away.
She lay on her left side, her right wing was stretched out
and upwards into a shattered tree. The skin like membrane
that made up the wing itself was punctured in several
places by sharp broken branches. Her great tail was bent
at an unnatural angle and was likely broken by the impact
of the crash. Several rows of puncture marks from the
two headed dragon's teeth ran down both sides as well. It
didn't look good. The other men from his troop arrived at
the scene. They exchanged hushed exclamations as they
saw the damaged trees, the dragon, and their leader. The
sergeant, with help from several of the men, carefully
rolled Jester over onto his back. The sergeant looked for
any blood or wounds and found nothing. "Well, you've
looked better I dare say, but you'll live to fight another
day." Jester swallowed and whispered. "Tantrus?" The
sergeant looked over his shoulder at the great dragon. Her
eyes were now open, and looking directly at him. Her gaze
was a little unsettling. He turned back to his friend and
cleared his throat. "She didn't do as well as you. Her right
wing and her tail are in bad shape. She is unable to move

much at all I'm afraid. The men can help her untangle her wing from the trees, but I'm not so sure we should try and move her just yet." Jester closed his eyes for a moment. "Sergeant, can you move me close to her?" The sergeant waved the men over. "This might hurt a little, are you sure you want to be moved?" "Jester crossed his eyes at the sergeant. The sergeant smiled and looked at the men gathered round him. "Right then, everyone grab a handful and we carefully move him to the dragon. On three. One, two, three." They gently lifted Jester off the ground and carried him to Tantrus. They placed him beside her head so she could see him. Jester looked at her and knew she was in some pain and unable to move. He placed his hand on her chin and rubbed her jaw. Her eyes closed and she seemed to relax a little. He told her she had done well and that he and the men would help her. He knew her tail was broken, along with the right wing. She would let them untangle her wing so she could be able to rest. Dragons do feel pain, but can block it temporarily. He found himself wishing Myra was here. She would know exactly what to do. He was about to instruct the sergeant to go ahead, when several dragons flew directly overhead. Several of the little dragons nearby, shot upwards through the broken trees and joined the ones that had just flown over. Suddenly there was a great blast of air as another large dragon settled in the broken trees. The sergeant stood. "Sir, its Myra. She's here!"

Myra slid from the base of the dragon's neck. She ran to Jester and knelt beside him, picking up his hand and holding it to her. "What has happened to you? Are you badly hurt?" Her eyes were moist with tears and she looked worried. "It was an unplanned landing. Less than graceful, I'm afraid." He squeezed her hand. "Tantrus needs your help more than I. She took the worst of it I'd say." Myra reached over Jester and rubbed the dragons jaw. "You were both lucky I think. I can help her. But I'm not so sure she will be able to fight with us." He strained and sat up finally. His breathing was getting easier now. Just then a muffled thump came from behind him, followed by a shower of pine needles and some trilling. Zara scrambled over top of him, wings outstretched so he couldn't see Myra. He managed a laugh and folded her wing so he could see again. Zara pushed against him, cat like, and settled in his lap. He felt better having both Myra and Zara with him. "So you think you can heal Tantrus?" He looked up at Myra. Even though she had just come to her senses, she was still the take charge woman he had come to love. "Yes, I'll need your help if you're up to it?" she said. He sat up fully and raised his eyebrows. "I'll do my very best my lady." he said formally. "Fine then, I'll need the men to hold her wing still, and some to remove the branches caught in it. Then carefully lower it to the ground. And you sir, need to keep rubbing her jaw so she stays relaxed. She will feel what we are doing to her" The sergeant turned to the men. "You heard her! Look lively now!" shouted the sergeant. Some men climbed into the wrecked tree that the big dragon's wing was impaled on. A few others climbed a nearby tree and got hold of her wing tip to steady it. Myra stood and leaned into Tantrus, reaching her forward right shoulder. She placed both hands onto the base of the damaged wing and closed her eyes. After a moment she turned to the sergeant and nodded. The men began cutting the branches with their swords. In a few moments the wing came free of the branches holding it. The men holding the wing strained against the weight, but managed to lower it to the ground carefully. "That's perfect sergeant. Now the tail. You'll need everyone you have to move it when I say." The sergeant and the men moved to the broken tail. They spread out along its length, ready to lift and swing it around straight. Myra leaned her body across the dragon's head and held her neck with both hands. The dragon closed her eyes and exhaled loudly. "Ok sergeant, swing it around strait as you can. Slow and steady if you will!" shouted Myra. The men got a good hold of the massive tail and began to swing it around carefully. Part way through the swing, a loud pop was heard. Everyone froze. "It's ok, keep going! Nice and straight if you can!" yelled Myra. They continued with their swing motion till the tail appeared straight as possible. "That's it! Stop there." shouted Myra. Tantrus felt hot now. Myra walked to the base of the dragon's tail and placed both hands firmly on the sides of the tail and closed her eyes again. She slowly moved both hands back towards the rear legs of the dragon and paused. The sergeant was still holding the tail midway along its length. He could feel the heat in the scales change to a coolness he remembered from the little ones who used him as a handy perch previously. He relaxed his hold on the tail and stood, marvelling at the transformation in Tantrus. He smiled at a job well done. A few months ago, he couldn't have imagined doing what he'd just done in his wildest dreams. He guessed his friend Jester had felt this way not long ago either. It was thanks to these creatures that they even had a fighting chance against Vectus. In that moment, he was changed forever, and a better man for it. Myra stood and moved across to the right wing. She gently touched the leathery skin that spanned the wing itself. She reached into her pocket in her grey dress and produced a stout heavy needle. "Sergeant, I'll need a horse blanket if you will." The sergeant looked around at the men. "Ives, fetch your blanket. You're used to not having it thanks to Jester and the Princess. Give it to her." The men laughed out loud. Ives did as he was told and presented his slightly scorched blanket to Myra. Even she laughed politely, remembering the day she was wrapped up into it. "I thank you my young man, it goes to a good cause, I assure you." Ives turned a bit red faced, and bowed deeply. His helmet slipped from his head and landed on his foot. He jumped up and down, then lost his balance and fell. Everyone laughed at that. Myra smiled at him, and then looked over at Jester. "I see you both share the same helmet maker!" Everyone laughed even harder. Jester laughed the hardest. It was his trademark 'Oooops'. Zara trilled loudly and stretched her wings out, flapping them in Jesters face. Tantrus turned her head and looked at Ives. She blew a huge smoke ring into the air. They all laughed again. She was definitely on the mend. Myra went to work on the damaged wing skin. After a while she had stitched the torn skin together and returned the remains of the horse blanket to Ives personally. "Thank you brave knight, your sacrifice shall not go unnoticed." stated Myra. Ives turned beet red at that. His horse blanket was a full third smaller than earlier. It was barely big enough for a pony. He placed it on his horse with great reverence. The men laughed again. He turned redder still, but he was happy to have helped the cause. When he was done he smiled back at everyone. The tiny blanket, now firmly on his brave horses back. Myra returned to Jester's side and knelt down in the leaves. "Ives is so like you, it's scary!" They both laughed at that.

Tantrus was finally able to relax fully. Her tail and right wing felt better. The damage was healing quickly and she longed to carry the fight to the blue skies above. Every now and then, a dragon would pass over head. She would look skyward and wish it was her. The dragon battle was in full swing as she lay there healing from the wounds sustained from the two headed dragon that Vectus rode. The one with the chains swinging from its legs, were a sad testament of Vectus himself. It was a complete absence of compassion for any living thing. Tantrus would bide her time. The awakening would come soon enough. This she knew.

The sergeant and Myra helped Jester to his feet. He felt his ribs carefully, and took a few steps. He was sore, but otherwise fit to carry on with the battle at hand. Jester looked at Myra. "Right then, Tantrus will heal thanks to you, but will she be able to fly in a day or two? Or should I find my horse?" asked Jester. "I wish I could say one way or the other. She was badly injured, but my magic is very powerful. Tantrus is a strong dragon, with a score to settle if she can. I think she could fly as early as tomorrow, but I can't be sure." she said. Several more dragons flew overhead, skimming the tree tops. A larger shadow passed a moment later, followed by two more. It was a group of two headed creatures controlled by Vectus. "I'm getting the feeling they are looking for us now. Vectus knows if he kills me, he'll have little resistance in the kingdom. Sergeant, how are the men faring on the beaches?" asked Jester. "We have been able bring down several dragons, but we are getting short on bolts and the bows. I'm glad we put backups in the trees. The dragon scale shields are holding up well, otherwise we would have to hide in the trees. In another day or so, we'll be unable to do much damage though." The sergeant regarded Jester. The battle was mostly a stalemate so far. Both sides had suffered some losses. They needed a game changer to force Vectus to abandon the invasion. Jester was about to speak when a great crashing in the trees overhead made them jump. A black two headed dragon landed heavily in the trees where Tantrus and Jester had crashed earlier. They all froze. The creature was huge and looked like it might attack at any moment. Its two heads seemed to writhe with pain as it tried to focus on the group of humans before it. Jester made a small movement with his right hand. His sword that had been dropped during the crash landing slid through the leaves and broken branches and gently lifted itself into his hand. Myra leaned into his ear. "How did you do that?" she asked incredulously. "Magnetic attraction I think" said Jester matter of factly. Myra smiled back at him, despite the danger of the dragon before them. The great beast hissed at them. Tantrus glared at the creature. One move and she would attack it, even in her present condition, she would protect Myra and Jester. Zara hissed back at the black dragon and spread her wings to appear slightly larger and slightly more fearsome. Even the dragon that Myra had ridden to them bared its teeth and stood its ground. The great dragon sat back on its haunches, unsure of what to do next. It surly would have attacked by now if it had been intent on killing them. Jester suddenly noticed the blackened chains attached to its legs! It was the dragon Vectus had ridden. He began a slow scan of the forest immediately around the crash site. As far as he could tell, the dragon arrived alone. He instinctively tightened his grip on his sword. His ears strained to hear the tiniest sound, but the forest was silent. Myra leaned into his ear again. She whispered, "Hold your sword to the dragon, blade downwards, I have an Idea." Slowly, Jester raised the sword as Myra had instructed. The sun flashed from the polished metal, he could feel a slight vibration in its handle. The black dragon became still and looked steadily at the sword, glimmering in the sunlight. Without any warning, Myra stepped from behind Jester and walked up to the two headed beast. The dragon lowered both of its head's towards her. Jester felt he would crush the sword's handle in his grip. Myra slowly raised her hands and placed them on both of the heads. She closed her eyes. The sergeant looked over at Jester, moving only his eyes. After a moment, Myra rubbed the jaws of both the dragon's heads. She turned towards Jester and the sergeant. "It wants to be free of Vectus. It wishes us no harm but cannot break the powerful grip he has on it. She has come alone. Vectus is resting, recharging the energy it takes to control these dragons. If we can get Vectus into a place we can overload his senses, the dragons can break free of his dark magic. They would be our allies in this fight. They only ask for their freedom from his powerful hold on them." She turned back to the dragon and replaced her hands on its heads. Zara trilled loudly and perched herself on Myra's shoulders. Jester slowly replaced his sword in its scabbard, and approached the dragon. He put his hands beside Myra's. He could feel the creatures desire to have freedom. It was not unlike any of the other dragons. He closed his eyes and communicated with it. They had been enslaved from birth by Vectus. Many had died while in his powerful grip. They were a breed apart but had no natural quarrel with human kind or other dragons for that matter. It was a question of forced ideals. Vectus wanted more than he already had. Total control of everything he could see, and what he could not. He would never rest until he attained domination over every living thing. Jester knew that Vectus was unstable. He needed to devise a way to overload him, enough that the black dragons could break free. It would be the end of Vectus, once and for all! Jester looked over at Myra. "I can only do this once I'm afraid." he said to Myra. She nodded. Jester carefully withdrew his sword again and placed the crest of it against the dragon's chest. He closed his eyes and willed the dark powers to leave this dragon. Fill it with light, and give it immunity to Vectus and his control. The sword vibrated and the dragon calmed even further. It was done. He hoped this dragon would be the beginning of

the end for Vectus and his dark powers. It would spread
the message to the others, even though still captive by the
dark powers, they would understand and wait for their
moment. Jester bent down and touched the gleaming
blade against the chains attached to its legs. They fell from
it without any resistance. Both Myra and Jester joined
the sergeant and the others at the opposite edge of the
tangled crash site. The great beast lifted upwards out of
the clearing with several powerful down beats of its wings
and turned towards the coast once more. The chains no
longer hanging from its legs. Jester looked at his sergeant.
"Have the men gather those chains. They are not finished
the job of providing restraint quite yet." He winked at
the sergeant. "Sir, do you trust the black dragon? It is
the one Vectus rides after all." "Yes, I certainly do now.
It's no longer being controlled against its will. All of the
black dragons have been enslaved by Vectus. None of
this is voluntary behaviour I assure you. Vectus has not
counted on finding a dragon master in Tyde. His takeover
of our kingdom is not going as planned. I think it will
continue to go poorly for him. The dragons in his control
wish to be free from his grasp and will do anything
they can to achieve that! I need to get to a dragon stone
again. Sergeant, you and the men remain with Myra and
Tantrus. Zara and I have some 'masonry' work to do."
Both Myra and the sergeant raised their eyebrows at that.
"Don't worry, I'll have help, now if you'll excuse me, I

have a dragon to catch." Jester winked at them and headed for the path to the beach. Zara trilled and ran after Jester.

As Jester strode down the path towards the nearby beach, he called for King to meet them at the tree line. King swung his huge head in the direction of the trees and began his heavy walk towards them. He had been eager to do more than sink a few ships earlier that day. Now he would assist the dragon master. He found Jester and Zara waiting at the tree line and lowered his head to him. Jester made his connection with him. It was important work to be done. Because of his size, King allowed Jester to grab onto a wingtip and then gently raised him up onto his huge back. The dragon master sat just forward of the base of the great dragon's neck. With several great down beats of his wings, King was clearing the tree tops and they were off to the dragon stone in the clearing near Jester's castle. Jester looked carefully around them, but no sign of Vectus yet. He had King fly over top his own castle and waved at the troops along the battlements. Zara was in her usual place in front of Jester, still wearing her copper armour. He smiled at that. She looked back at him and trilled. He rubbed her jaw line as they made the steep turn to land in the clearing. Jester slid from Kings huge back and landed heavily in the grass. He found the edges of the nearly sunken stone and began digging along the sides. King grunted and placed both of his front feet on the stone. Jester rolled off to the side as King's powerful forelegs easily pulled the stone clear of the ground. He stood there and stared. He then ran round to the wing tip and was boosted onto the dragons back. In moments they were off again, with the massive stone safely in Kings grip. They flew northwest, towards Dunvegan Manor. As they approached the manor, Jester had King make a very low pass directly in front of the library window. He could clearly see Sir Dunvegan open mouthed at King clutching the dragon stone beneath him as they then turned sharply towards the open stony hill behind Myra's place.

They circled the hill top several times, and then landed in the lightening scorched circle. Jester had King raise the stone fully upright so it stood in the center. It was the perfect place for the largest dragon stone in the kingdom. When the stone was set, he had King take him back to the crash site. Before king left he had given him instructions to begin piling firewood around the inside of the circle, leaving some gaps for the humans to enter safely. King left in a hurricane of leaves and small twigs. Jester came over to Myra who was sitting next to Tantrus. "I have an idea." he said. Myra looked at him with raised eyebrows and smiled.

Chapter Twenty

(The ending of a beginning)

It was very late in the afternoon when it started. The black dragons of Ionicus began wave after wave of attacks on the various castles and farms in the kingdom. Fire and dense smoke rose skyward as far as the eye could see. From time to time, an occasional black dragon would fall from the sky, a victim of the three on one attack's from the dragons of Tyde. Jester, along with Myra, Sir Dunvegan, and his sergeant and men, had arrived at the top of the rocky barren hill top. The huge dragon stone now at its center, and firewood piled around the circular lightening burn. The sun was arcing downwards towards its end of day. Jester walked over to the dragon stone and faced everyone. He looked directly at Myra and spoke. "This is your marker, remember it well. For one day it will surely save your life. These were the words said to me by this most wonderful of all Princesses. As you can see, I've not forgotten the words, but their meaning finally came to me earlier today. It is here we make a final stand with the darkness that is Vectus. Tonight will see the final outcome of this new invasion of our lands and perhaps our very way of life. Easy words, difficult task. Perhaps not all who stand here now with me will survive this night. The dangers are many and terrifying. I ask that you all stand with me in this special place tonight. It is here that we will defeat Vectus and put an end to the dark power he holds over every living thing. As the sun drops below the horizon and night falls upon us, we will begin the ending. The dragons have their plan now, and I trust everyone standing here will be true to its outcome. This is not a traditional battle as you know. Nor will it be a traditional defeat of the darkness that will come upon us. Every one of us must stand true in our trust and belief in not only our God, who will watch over us, but in ourselves. This battle will not be won with sword and arrows alone, but on faith. Faith in God, faith in ourselves, and faith in our fellow countrymen. The dark power is strong but not as strong as our faith. Combined with our dragon brothers I believe we have the upper hand in this stand we make tonight. May none of you falter, but take strength in our desire for freedom and equality for all. Together we all stand as one tonight." He paused and then walked back to Myra, her father, and his sergeant. "It is begun." he stated simply.

The sun had set as it had since the beginning of time. A dull orange colored afterglow remained in the sky. Fires could be seen for miles around as the black dragons continued their attacks. "What exactly are the plans for the dragons." asked Dunvegan. Jester merely extended his arms outwards towards the darkened land. "Keep watching." he said. Everyone on the hill top looked out onto the land below. For a few moments nothing changed at all. Then, one by one, the fires began to go out. A few at first, then more and more followed. After a long while the last of the fires was extinguished. The land in all directions was black again. Everyone turned to Jester and looked at him in amazement. He turned to his sergeant. "Have the men light the wood piles now." Pile after pile of dry wood was set ablaze within the circle. A second circle much further away from the lightening circle suddenly erupted in flames. "Now we wait...we wait for the moth to come to the flame." Jester crossed his arms as he stood in front of the dragon stone.

The two massive rings of fire could be seen for miles. Vectus spotted them as he was trying to see why all the burning had suddenly stopped. His dragons had begun burning everything when suddenly all the fire had gone out. This was a strange thing to happen, even for him. From the perch on his dragons back, he could clearly see the two fire rings in the distance. Something was up and he would soon put an end to it. This kingdom would burn for weeks in his own plans, now the fires had gone out. Angered by this, he began a fast descent towards the burning rings. He ordered his two headed beasts to follow. He made a wide pass over the flames and could see many troops down below within the inner ring of fire. Obviously the first to offer themselves in death no doubt. There was a large gap in the flames in the inner circle. He landed away outside the gap. Hundreds more of his black dragons landed in the wide space between the flaming circles and stood wing to wing completely surrounding the inner circle. Vectus dismounted his dragon and took several steps towards the gap in front of him. This was too easy he thought. A simple wave from his right hand would command his dragons to burn every living thing within to ash in just moments.

Vectus could just make out a lone figure ahead of him. Standing before a tall narrow stone of some kind. He strode past the gap in the burning inner ring and realized it was the dragon master of Tyde before him. Nice. He would kill him as easily as all the others gathered there. He noticed the woman near him as the one he had captured earlier, along with an old man beside her. All three stood with their arms crossed facing him. He knew the old man was the shielder, the one who held the dark powers at bay. He smiled knowing all who were important to this kingdom were in one place. A foolish mistake. Perhaps they were gathered here to offer a truce or surrender. There would be no such thing. His smile widened slightly. He was aware of his dragons shuffling outside the inner ring of fire. He guessed they were anxious to begin the final burning of the occupants of the hill top. They would get their way soon enough. Vectus took several steps forward and stopped. He glared at Jester, still standing before the dragon stone.

"Dragon master, we meet yet again. I see in your unplanned, and under thought stupidity you have given me the gift of all your deaths in one easy stroke. That was most thoughtful of you I must admit. I hope you are prepared for it." Jester held up his hands palms up. "Vectus, your arrogance amazes even me. You think you can just show up and take this kingdom for your own? You failed to take a lesson learned from the last time you set foot here. Your dark powers have failed you since you first took them for your own. I offer you this once, and once only. You may return to Ionicus unharmed if you leave quietly now. Your dragons will remain with us and any men you have left may remain if they wish to." Vectus looked around him. "Are you talking to me? Do you really know who I am? How dare you address me in that manner! I will save you for last dragon master of Tyde." Vectus pulled a short dagger from his waist and threw it to the ground with such force it stuck into the solid rock like it was soft earth. He glared again at Jester and spat beside the knife imbedded in the rock.

Jester turned to his sergeant. "Sergeant, I believe this man has broken the law here in Tyde. No one is permitted to spit in a public place. It's punishable by a stay in our jail overnight with out food I'll add." The sergeant nodded. "You want me to arrest this common law breaker?" said the sergeant. "Not now sergeant. I think he has more laws to break before he is through with us. I'll allow him to play a little longer before we take him into custody." Jester winked at the sergeant. Vectus was incensed by this. They are all about to die, and they make light of him and his purpose here. Vectus took several long strides towards Jester. He drew his sword and held it before him. Vectus was repelled by the brilliance of the light shining forth from the sword. He staggered backwards several steps, his hands up before him shielding his eyes. "Fool, you think a highly polished sword can stop me?" He was about to turn and walk away from the inner ring of fire when the flames went out. Vectus stopped in his tracks. He looked for his dragons beyond the inner ring. They were no longer present. In there place was several hundred little green dragons. He knew they were the ones responsible for sinking his fleet and killing his own dragons. Zara hissed at him and made a smoke ring that lazily encircled his feet. Vectus stared at her. "Is that all you can do? You're a waste of dragon scales. I'll crush the life out of you before your next breath!" As Vectus made a move towards Zara, the smoke ring ignighted. A powerful flash of blue flame engulfed him, then went out. He hissed back at Zara, she only stared back at him quietly. He turned back to Jester. "Is this all you can bring to bear. This is a child's birthday party!" The veins on his neck stood out in sharp relief. "It's time to die dragon master!" He took a step towards him and the pile of burning logs behind the great stone exploded, revealing two more stones similar to the tall one but smaller. Myra and her father each went to a stone and made their connection to it. A brilliant light began to shine upwards from the three stones, then the light radiated outwards, it was dazzling to the eyes. Vectus felt a tremor in the ground behind him. He quickly turned and came face to face with Tantrus. The child's birthday party was becoming more adult now. He stepped backwards a few steps. Zara fluttered onto his left shoulder and perched there. The bluish white light emanated from the stones and shone brightly over what seemed like the whole kingdom. Jester's sword glowed with a light of its own. The rays of light were blinding Vectus. His eyes felt as if they were being burned from the inside outwards. For the first time since childhood he felt true fear. A panic was building within him. He tried to look past the blinding

light but was disoriented. He could not control the light
that burned his vision. He brought all his dark powers
to bear and just wanted the light to stop. It didn't work.
He staggered backwards till he bumped into Tantrus
and froze. Where were the black creatures he'd enslaved
with his great power? Suddenly he saw his 'own' dragon
behind the dragon master. It was protecting him, the
woman, and the old man. The other black dragons stood
just outside the inner circle. In between each one was
a full size dragon of Tyde. The black dragons had now
sided with them! They had turned somehow. This was
not possible! He had total control of everything! This
could never happen! Vectus closed his eyes and tried to
regain his composure, but it was not forthcoming. His
fear gripped him like a jacket of ice. He grabbed Zara by
the neck and threw her to the ground, then dived towards
his dagger stuck into the stone and pulled it free. With a
quick look, he threw the knife with all his might towards
Jester and the great stone. His aim was too high. His 'own'
dragon caught the knife in its mouth and shot it back at
him. In amazement, he watched the knife shoot straight
at him. It passed through his helmet and buried itself to
the hilt in his forehead. Jester stepped towards Vectus
and looked into Vectus's eyes and said, "This is your end.
You and your dark powers are finished. The balance is
restored now. What you completely forgot about in your
insanely arrogant plans is that things like hope, love,

and faith still have the ability to overpower any sense of
control you thought you had. You are no longer, return
from whence you came." At that, Tantrus took his head
in her great jaws and bit through his neck. A greasy black
smoke came from his neck and Zara made another smoke
ring and ignighted it. Jester stepped back. It was over.
Tantrus took off from the hill top with Vectus's head still
in her jaws. All of the other dragons followed her. They all
climbed to a great hight. Tantrus finally dropped the head
from her jaws. As the head fell back towards the hill top
she let loose with her hottest flame. Every other dragon
in the kingdom followed suit. By the time the head
would have struck the ground, it was mere ash. The early
morning breeze scattered it into the reseeding darkness.
The invasion was over and would never come again. Jester
realized the sun rise was just beginning. A new dawn
began in Tyde, one without smoke and fire. One with
out fear of a future invasion from Ionicus. Jester felt an
arm around him. It was Myra. "We did it! It's done." She
hugged him close. Zara flew to his shoulder and flapped
her wings excitedly. The sergeant and Sir Dunvegan
cheered and shook hands. The men of Jester's troop finally
sat and were able to relax. As Jester hugged Myra he
suddenly froze. "What on earth is that?" Myra turned and
followed his gaze. Coming up the hill was a horse with a
too small blanket, pulling a vendors cart. It was followed
by several others. Two men walked beside the horse. It

was Ives and the sausage and bun vendor from his castle. Myra smiled and said to no one in particular, "You've got to be kidding me…" "Well, I don't know about you, but I'm suddenly very hungry! You have to try this new food. Breakfast is on me." said Jester. Zara flapped her wings excitedly and trilled. The sun's first rays struck the dragon stones and the distant forest came alive with the sounds of birds and the other creatures. The day had begun as it had for millennia.

The End

About the Author

Imagination is the mind's four-wheel drive. It can allow us to create things both real and imaginary. I have always had a great imagination and wanted to write this book as time permitted. Imagination can bring you along on any journey, including others. Between a book's cover is the guideline to take us to places both real and imagined. The power of a story well told takes us right there. It's a wonderful experience! It is these journeys that I enjoy most.

This is my first book project, and I have enjoyed every moment spent writing. Now I hope the reader enjoys every moment reading.

I'm a Canadian living in Southern Alberta, in the shadow of the Rockies. It's a beautiful land of extreme weather, though. I've made plans to relocate to the Dominican Republic in mid 2015. I look forward to a much kinder climate and a simpler lifestyle.